DYLAN BASSETT

GAD'S
BOOK

Outpost19 | San Francisco
outpost19.com

Bassett, Dylan
Gad's Book / Dylan Bassett
ISBN 9781944853853

Available in paperback and ebook editions.

OUTPOST19

ORIGINAL PROVOCATIVE
SAN FRANCISCO | @OUTPOST19

More advance praise

"Gad's Book is a haunting novel of violence, paranoia and delusion, of a splintering consciousness in
a hellscape much like today—wildly inventive, desperate, deft, painfully funny, and in the end, nothing
short of brilliant."

—Elizabeth McKenzie

DYLAN BASSETT

GAD'S BOOK

That man. Something about him. Something wrong. He made a face like he wanted to have sex with everything he looked at, and he looked at everything. He cocked back his head to simulate height, so that the eyes seemed to point down on the object of their gaze.

Now he looked at me.

Now he opened his hand and extended his arm and told me to sit. Down, he said.

And I did.

That was the beginning of all my problems. The first of my last days in California.

PART ONE

I was still living in the Midwest when, on a winter morning, I woke up and didn't know who I was. Black eye. Cut lip. Broken tooth. Blood. All over the pillow and sheets and carpet. I thought it was someone else's. It was smeared on the wall in the shape of a crescent moon. Who's been bleeding on me?

Joe, my housemate—muscular guy with a manbun—was standing over me, covering his mouth.

I'd had a seizure, he told me. I'd been sleepwalking. I'd kicked a chair over, made an obscene gesture, punched Joe in the neck, called him a snakebitch, and threatened to call the police if he didn't bring me a beer.

Good Lord, he said. What are you repressing?

In the following weeks, I had the sense that someone or something had been tinkering with my memory, remapping my consciousness, reprogramming my thoughts. I had the thought that I should go to sleep and try never to wake up. The thought that the universe was contracting. The thought that the human soul was the weight of a baby. The thought that I was growing a very small penis in my armpit. The thought that aliens were colonizing my brain, my thoughts, my speech.

Then I had another seizure. And then another.

I went to the emergency room and, a few hours later, met with a neurologist. He shined a light in my eye and said—in a heavy German accent—look at my finger. My finger, over here. He poked my knee and said touch your nose. He put his hand on my neck and on my lower back and said breathe, breathe. He touched my shoulder, my elbow. He lifted my arm. Cough, he said. Blink. Blink faster. He said to remember these words: orange, airplane, bulldog. He told me that I seemed stressed. He said, stress and sleep deprivation are triggers for seizures. You should probably give up coffee and alcohol, too.

But I'm writing a novel, I said. I need coffee, at least.

Maybe you should lay off the novel for a while.

I didn't know what to say.

Now. Can you repeat the words I told you?

Orange. Bulldog. Airplane.

Orange. *Airplane*. Bulldog.

Isn't that what I said?

After three EEGs and two MRIs, I was diagnosed with nocturnal epilepsy and put on a heavy dose of something I still can't remember how to pronounce.

After that, the world was traced in thick black lines. I had the sense that reality was lurking just behind my immediate experience. Everything seemed intense, but I couldn't quite access that intensity. I wanted to. I wanted to live again. A new life.

Okay, I thought. No more cynicism. No

more freezing winters.

So, I planned my escape.

I called Parker, a friend from graduate school who had moved to Oakland, California a few years earlier to work as a marketer at one or another tech company.

He took my call.

Parker, I said.

Long time, he said.

I want to get out of here, I said. I want to go west.

He called me an idiot.

I want to be inspired. I want to practice the unironic religion of myself.

He laughed and called me an idiot again. *West* is a bad word, you know. No one says that word anymore unless they mean to say something bad.

I asked him questions about moving to California. What do I have to do to get there?

It's too late, he said. You missed the boat. California used to be a cure for sadness. Now, it's the saddest state in the country. Look it up. Everyone is lonely and stressed out and scared and mad about something.

Can you help me? I said.

A few weeks later, Parker called a friend of a friend and hooked me up with a job as a copywriter at a startup. And you can work from home, he said. Huge perk.

I had an old truck, a small thing. Most of the time, I was embarrassed to admit that it was mine—embarrassed by the way it lunged forward, by the way it sputtered and spit. There was no need to drive it, really. Not until now. Now I was on my way. I took it down I-80, slow as it went, all the way to California.

Six months later and summer was already over. I couldn't tell the difference. The weather was fine, but that meant nothing in that part of the world, where every day was hot or cold or luke-warm—whatever time of year—and the days did not follow logically one after the other and things changed so fast they seemed not to change at all.

That afternoon, I did what I tended to do when I knew what I was doing. I walked to the Writer's Block bookstore, where I planned to sit and work on the novel I hadn't been writing. I went north on Telegraph Avenue, taking my good time and stopping in a few intervening shops, including the coffee nook where I bought an espresso I didn't need, and the CVS where I picked up the anti-depressants I wasn't taking and the seizure medication I was scared to take, and Joe's Smoke Shop where I bought cigarettes I didn't smoke but carried visibly in my shirt pocket and occasionally held between my thumb and pointer fingers so as to be seen holding them.

Telegraph Avenue was very old and very new. Even now, months after moving to Berkeley, I was possessed by the clatter of it; by the street vendors selling athleisure, "mom jeans for non-moms," Forever Pants, crop tops, floral blouses, and Blundstone rustic boots; by the rumble of bicycles, skateboards, and car horns; by the rows of bakeries, boutique kiosks, popup gift shops selling hippie and post-hippie kitsch; by the stacks of used books and the bins of records for sale outside of stores that didn't otherwise sell books or records; by the tastefully grungy health food stores stocked with organic everything. Grass-fed, grass-finish. Local beets and onions and knob celery and sunchoke and Brussels berry sprout and yard-long beans. Yogurt from mother's milk. Yogurt from synthetic alternative milk. Guac-Kale-Mole. Vegetable milk. Veganic Sprouted Ancient Maize Flakes. Edible Flowers. Kelp Granules. Wild Salmon Skin. Raw. Unadulterated. Straight-from-the-hive. Root juice. Bean Sauce. Sauce Box. Boxed Water. Pumpkin Spice Rice Milk. Beer Wine. Sparkling Wine Water.

A dusty light cut the late-morning haze and lit the edges of the brick buildings and the white adobe buildings and the featureless glass buildings that looked like an archaic vision of the future. The people came out, and more were coming. There were transients, huddled around the benches and alleyways, with threadbare tents and dogs. There were students and artists, the new free-spirits who resembled the old free-spirits. There were tech types with their heads in gadgets. And there were tourists—voyeurs, like me, to the spectacles and specters of radical culture, to the ghosts of the city's past, now preserved and reproduced in splashy simulacrum. The street had the bloated, overwrought qualities of a parody—a pastiche of the golden era of free-thinking and free love.

I opened my photo app and practiced

making my faces into its camera—the ones I planned to wear for whoever looked at me. I wore boots without socks, and my pants rolled tightly up, a white t-shirt under a faded eggshell button-up under a Zara boyfriend blazer. I wanted my disheveled appearance to seem natural, careless, too casual to evoke a sense of fashion—enough to warrant attention, but not full scrutiny. I felt like I was pretending to be what I already was: a good citizen, if that was possible—polite and agreeable, a nonthreatening everyday taxpayer who said the right things. I wore an old wristwatch, fastened backward, upside-down, around my arm so that the dial sat on the inside of my wrist, and I flipped my hand over to see it, open-closed-open. It was a woman's watch—or so I had been told—with a thin strap and a small greenish face. But it did not tell time because it was broken: the hands showed twelve, always twelve, midnight or noon. I don't know where I got it. I don't remember getting it. Maybe I found it or took it by mistake. Point was, I liked to wear it, to feel it there. It mattered to me. The thing of it. The evidence of something else.

•

When I arrived at the bookstore, the glass door was heavy, and I had to pull the hospital-style handle with both hands to exert enough strength to pry it from its latch. I went down the small flight of stairs toward the reading table in the corner where the novel section was.

Most days, that area was empty. But not

today. Today, a man was already there, sitting in the same place I usually sat—in the chair that leaned against the back wall where the entire bookshop could be observed.

It was him. That man. The one with the face.

I did not approach the table. Not yet. I tried to look at him without looking. I tried to stop looking. It didn't matter. He was everywhere. All torso and shoulders. Like a soldier. Built for a uniform. He had a beard and a thick braid that fell below his neckline. His frame was clad in faded black—his jeans were black, his T-shirt, his hair. I recognized what we had in common: an ambiguous complexion, a vague makeup. He could have been Turkish—of Turkish descent, like me. Or he could have been Spanish, Italian, southern French, Northern African, a certain kind of Welsh. Maybe Russian, eighteenth-century Russian, southern Russian, not exactly Russian per se, but maybe of the Baltic region. He could have been Greek, maybe, or Algerian, Egyptian, Brazilian, Brazilian-German.

Look. Don't look. He was reading, hunched over a gigantic book that looked worn by wear or water, and when he turned the pages—gold leaf, onionskin—it sounded like the paper was being torn. And he turned them anxiously, as if reading with pleasure or hatred, as if acting out the content of his reading, and the accumulation of torn pages sounded like he was destroying the book, tearing it apart page by page.

Now it was too late. Nothing else for me to do. I approached. Slowly at first, slower now, to avoid drawing attention to myself. I took the back of the chair opposite him and pulled it away from the table at an angle so as not to sit across from him directly.

He looked up like an animal from drinking. He waved his hand. Like that. Go ahead, he said. Take it.

I slid into the chair and set my bag on the table and took out my laptop and opened the screen.

Now the man was looking at my bag. Now at me. Now at my bag. Now at me. He kept his head that way—cocked, as if waiting for me to notice him, as if wanting to say something, or waiting, maybe, for an opportunity to interject without completely interrupting whatever he thought I was doing.

He twirled his beard.

I didn't look.

He cleared his throat.

I didn't look.

He exhaled. Hey, he said. Look. He pointed at me. We share something. The same design.

I was confused. Wait, I said. So, you *are* Turkish?

What? he said.

Oh, you're Welsh?

What?

What?

What?

Nothing. Never mind.

He pointed at my bag. Your bag, he said. I'm talking about that, your bag.

I looked down at the thing he was calling my bag—a canvas tote. It wasn't my bag, not really. I'd taken it from a lost-and-found on campus a few weeks earlier when I happened to walk by. I saw it on a shelf and said, Hey, that's my bag, the tote. And just like that, the kid behind the counter gave it up. Now I worried that the bag belonged to this man and that he'd accuse me of stealing it, or worse: that he'd threaten me if I didn't return it, that he'd cause a scene about it—shame me, call me out for theft, embarrass me to the point of being unable to return to this bookstore.

Oh. The bag? You can have it, I said politely—so politely, I think, that I worried I might have come off as condescending and sarcastic, that I might have been perceived to say precisely the opposite of what I meant.

His face changed—big grin—and he leaned forward. No, he said. I'm one of you. He kept on grinning like that. His grin grew ghastly. It evolved into a full-blown smile. A wide gap appeared between the top and bottom rows of teeth, and, for a moment, I thought he was going to scream. I'm one of you, he repeated. The arrows. Those. He pointed.

I didn't know anything about any arrows. I examined the bag, turning it over and back again, and yes—there, in the bottom right corner was an almost undetectable image. A small sewn-on patch: three skinny arrows pointing downward at a slant.

Now the man pulled his collar down to show me a tattoo on his neck. It was the same

10

symbol. Three arrows. Now he made a fist and extended it toward me for a bump. I bumped it.

I looked at my wristwatch and pretended to think about something and went back to writing and not writing my novel.

We sat like this for a while. Writing. Not writing. I glanced at him to see whether he was glancing at me and caught him glancing to see if I might be glancing at him, and on one occasion, he looked up from his reading and made a surprised face directly at me, as if I were reading the same book and wanted to know whether I was thinking the same thing he had been thinking.

I looked away. He looked away. I looked at him. He looked back.

Now he hiccuped. He hiccuped again. I ignored him and typed something something on my computer. I was trying to write—something something something—but he kept on hiccuping, although hiccuping was not the right word for what he was doing. It was more like grunting, inhaling through his nose and forcing out a semi-verbal spasm that went, Neh. To hear the hiccup was almost to see it: to look right down into the man's throat, to watch his esophagus swell and shut. And he went on doing it, never excusing himself, so that the act seemed habitual, natural even—a compulsory expression of some internal, bodily crisis both involuntary and cultivated.

Because silence between us was so frequently marked by looking and not looking at each other, it felt like we were having a conversation, or that we should be having a conversation. And then finally he spoke. He said, so. Just like that. *So.* So, he said, what are you? A student? What? A techie?

A writer, I said.

A writer?

I mean, I said, I work as a *copywriter* for a startup. But I also write.

He clicked his tongue as if to summon a dog. What do you write?

I'm trying to write a novel, I let myself say.

Neh. He grinned again, and again I thought he was going to scream. Is your novel about a thirty-something living in Berkeley who writes a novel about a thirty-something living in Berkeley?

Well—.

Do writers write about anything other than themselves nowadays? Do they have visions?

The sun hung in the back window and a concentration of heat settled on top of me. I was sweating in my jogger pants. I wiped my forehead with my t-shirt sleeve. I pulled at my crotch and changed the subject. What are you reading? I looked again at my wristwatch to show that I didn't really care but wanted to be polite.

He held up his book to show me. The Holy Bible. King James. I'm reading Ezekiel, he said.

Ezekiel, I said. What's Ezekiel's story?

Ezekiel is a messenger of God in the final days of Jerusalem, he said—and that's how he talked, all direct and present tense. He went on. Ezekiel is called to preach before the Babylonian empire demolishes the city and desecrates the temple. To warn the Jerusalemites of their coming destruction, Ezekiel wanders into the desert and performs a series of prophetic acts. He plucks out every single strand of hair on his head. He pulls them out one by one and scatters them around the ground and burns the follicles of hair and he lies on his left side for three hundred and ninety days and makes bread with his own excrement and vomit and eats it and survives.

I tugged at my crotch again. He makes bread with excrement?

His own poop, yeah. And eats it.

I don't get it.

What don't you get?

Why does he do that?

To prove something.

To prove that you can make bread out of poop?

To prove the destruction of the city, he said. To prove it true. He wants to show the people what suffering looks like. He wants them to see it. All the confusion and fear of the moment, you know. Images are the highest form of communication. Words are no good.

He went on, droning in a deep voice like a poet reading on the radio. So, he said, Jerusalem is sacked. Vast numbers of people. Slaughter and bloodshed and pandemonium and war. Capture. Torture. Starvation. Cannibalism. And Ezekiel has a vision of the heavens. He sees the sky open. Four beings descending. Each with four faces. Man, lion, ox, eagle. Four and four. And each has four wings. And their wings beat and make the sound of water crashing against the shores of a thousand nations. And their wings are gold, and they have the feet of oxen. And the whole body is covered in eyes, the hands, arms, legs—all of it. Thousands of watchful eyes. Enough eyes to watch the entire earth. And the wings go up and up, and the vision follows. And there is a throne of fire. The embodiment of light. The apocalyptic throne where death himself sits.

Silence.

What was I supposed to say to that? I had nothing. I couldn't think. I said: God. The word came right out of me, as if spoken by another. God, I said, works in mysterious ways.

He made a blank face.

Why did I say that? Mysterious ways? Does God work in mysterious ways? I was embarrassed to say it, and my embarrassment turned into panic, and in that panic, I devised not one explanation for my outburst, but three, and because I could not decide which of these explanations would be more believable, I said all of them, one after the other: I need to get to work, I said. I have a doctor's appointment. It's my turn to make dinner, and I need to get to the grocery store. I forgot. Completely forgot.

He looked at me for a moment—head back—and then waved his hand as if performing a magic trick and gathered up his belongings and stuffed his book and notebook and pen into a leather shoe bag. I'll walk you out, he said. I told him he didn't have to do that, but he was already up, next to me. He put his hand on me and looked down at my forehead.

We walked outside but before I could walk away he proposed a smoke—a genial smoke, he called it, among friends, real quick, quick smoke. Like Ishmael and Queequeg.

Thanks, but I don't smoke.

He pointed. You have cigarettes.

Oh. Right. I looked down and felt naked. Here. I opened the pack and extended a cigarette to him and he took it and lit it and put it in his mouth.

I held up mine with two fingers, thumb and pointer, and let him light it, and sucked and coughed and pretended to smoke without letting the thing really touch my lips.

Now he pointed his head up and made a face and cocked back his head like a bird and pushed his tongue out and blew smoke out in strange and contorted shapes—shapes of twisted bodies, disfigured limbs, deformed animals. A jellyfish, an elephant.

Sunlight fell the color of a low-grade infection on the grass and the withered trees and the foggy windows of the adjacent yoga studios that ran lengthwise along the street.

What's your name? he said.

I said my name.

I'm Lawson, he said. Zeke Lawson.

Wait. I almost laughed. *Your* name is Ezekiel?

He showed his teeth. That's right.

When we said goodbye, I asked him, out of politeness, I guess, for his phone number. I didn't want his phone number—not really—so I was

15

relieved when he told me that he didn't have a phone.

You don't have a phone? I didn't know there were still real people in the world without phones.

He didn't laugh.

And with that, he turned and went away. I thought I'd never see him again. But one month later, I did.

3

I walked away at a jog. I went in circles. My legs swelled. I didn't need to walk anywhere, I admit. And I had a bike that I rode when I remembered I had one. But mostly I preferred walking. I like to feel it, the swelling.

I was thinking of other things. My mind conjured up images: a jellyfish, an elephant. It conjured the image of the arrows. Three arrows. What did they mean? My mother had a tattoo of a quiver of arrows on her ankle. It means fellowship, she had said. Friendship. But whose friendship? A single arrow might symbolize, I don't know. On a street sign an arrow indicates direction, angled motion: turn, go ahead. There, and there only. But these arrows pointed down. Down? Thomas Pynchon, maybe? I took out my phone and googled "three arrows," and clicked the search icon. Three arrows, the phone told me: the anti-fascist political symbol. Antifa. Three arrows to represent the struggle against fascism, reaction, and capitalism. There it was. Was that it? So, the dude was a member of Antifa. So what?

•

I had lived in the same place since moving to Berkeley—a single room inside a tall Victorian-style house. I lived with eleven housemates but didn't know them. I hadn't managed more than a hello or a head nod in passing to any of them. I heard them talking outside my room. I heard them hooting and singing and stomping their feet. But I never saw them.

I happened to rent the room closest to the front door—a room that used to be a shared living space but had been turned into a "studio apartment" so the landlord could add another tenant, which may or may not have been legal. The location of the room allowed me to sneak in and out of the house undetected. Each time I entered, I held my breath and paused before the front door to make sure no one else was walking out. I kept my head down and lowered the top of my hood or hat to hide my face.

It wasn't that I didn't want to meet my housemates. It was only that, for the first few weeks after moving in, I didn't happen to see them. And I wasn't actively trying to meet them now, several months after moving in, because I suspected that, by doing so—introducing myself, acting sociable and good-natured—I might appear self-absorbed, presumptuous, overeager. I worried, in other words, that I might appear to be the opposite of what I intended to be. And, by this point, I thought I'd missed my opportunity to meet them, and I felt too awkward to try to meet them now; and I thought that if I *did* try to meet them now, they would want to know why I hadn't met them sooner. Probably, I thought, they had already made assumptions about me—that I was quiet, anti-social, perverted, maybe—and they would be looking for clues to confirm these speculations. Maybe they would notice things about me they wouldn't have noticed otherwise. Bad things. How I rocked on my heels when I didn't know what to say. How I stuttered. How I laughed when I was supposed to scoff. How I said the word *interesting* as a hedge against more thoughtful commentary. And maybe they would mistake my passive attitude for snobbery or indifference.

Presently I crept into my room and locked the door and turned on the overhead and—remembering an article in the NYT about the feel-good effects of "warm" light—turned it off again, and turned on, in its place, the desk light.

Cozy.

My housemates gathered in the kitchen now. I heard them. They were eating and drinking and laughing and slamming their glasses and knives and forks on the table.

The phone in my pocket vibrated. *After last week's ICE raids, his family still doesn't know where he is. An explosion in Russia killed five elite nuclear scientists and the government's secrecy fuels speculation about the cause. Several dogs died last week after exposure to blue-green algae. Violent crime skyrockets in America's biggest cities: up 30% in San Francisco. A new study finds we're not seeing reality, our vision runs 100 milliseconds behind the physical world.*

I made a vegan burrito in the microwave, which sat atop the mini-refrigerator next to the window. I sat at my desk and ate. I noted the similarity between the vegan "cheese" in the burrito and actual cheddar cheese. It was such an uncanny similarity, in fact, that I forced myself to dig into the trash and retrieve the burrito's individual packaging. I read the ingredients, and, it turned out, the burrito was only a regular microwave burrito with real cheddar cheese. It didn't matter. I wasn't a vegan, anyway. I just wanted people to like me.

Now I went to the window. The glass, with no light behind it, produced an anonymous mirror, the kind you find in hotel rooms: reflecting anonymity. I opened the latch and took out a cigarette and held it with my thumb and pointer finger and waved it around as if someone were watching. I smelled it and waved it around again. I felt awkward—although I was alone—acting like the person I thought I wanted to be.

I paced. I hovered around my bookshelf and looked over the stack of books I wasn't reading—*War and Peace, Crime and Punishment, Don Quixote*—and turned off the lights and got in bed and began to scour the internet. Hours passed. Hours and hours. Outside, the fog rose in concentric circles and the moonlight dispersed unevenly and produced a vague, mystifying filter.

What happened next happened quickly, within the span of a few minutes, and yet it seemed, in my mind, to fill the entire evening.

I was still in bed when I heard an uproar of voices—unintelligible and rhythmic and warlike. The chanting blended into a collective slur, shouting indistinctly into a megaphone. It moved—three blocks away, then two, then one, then two, three, four, closer and farther away—a marching band or a mob, coming from the north, now the south, southwest, west. Now the collective voice gathered up again and dispersed.

And now it happened.

A gunshot. I had to say it out loud to believe it. *That was a gunshot*. One shot. Now another. And another. I heard it like a knock at my window. Like an intruder outside of my room pounding on the glass, trying to get inside. Three knocks.

Is this happening?

Now someone cried out. Now police sirens. Someone yelled. Someone else was running. Now quiet again, no police sirens even. Nothing. The silence was therapeutic. I could hear myself hearing it. No one was screaming. There was no one there to scream.

The room reappeared and I heard my own heavy breathing. I reached for my phone, anticipating a call or a text message to come through, but the screen was dark. I thought to call someone, Parker maybe. But I worried that a call might signal my presence, my location; and that it might draw the wrong kind of attention.

Was it a gunshot?

No, idiot. It was a firecracker. It was a backfiring motorcycle. A nail gun, maybe. Maybe a heavy object falling. You don't even know what a gun sounds like. You've never heard gunfire in your life. On television or YouTube, okay, but not in real life.

Where were my roommates? Why wasn't anyone moving? Why couldn't I hear them?

What I wanted was to rewind the scene

and listen again—to hear another gunshot. Yes, I wanted the gun to fire one more time. Or no. I didn't want that exactly, but I wanted to listen to it a fourth time, to be sure that it had been what I thought it was. I googled what does a gun sound like. I googled gunshots, loud gunshots, louder gunshots. I listened to the sound over and over. I googled rifle, shotgun, machine-gun, revolver, Glock.

I sat up and went and looked out the window to see what was happening beyond the glass. The street was empty—and it was because of this emptiness, I suddenly felt an undeniable presence. Some dim seer, out of sight, looking in. I dropped down to the floor to hide and lifted my head to see. I rationalized that what I was feeling was only the lingering effect of having been with that man. Big guy with the Bible. Zeke. He had made an impression so singular that I had carried it with me from the bookstore to the room, and I had projected it there.

A knot tightened.

It's the bag. The tote. I said it out loud. Throw it out. Get rid of it. I snatched the thing and shook it clean over my desk and set it in the trash-can and stomped it down and stomped again.

For the rest of the night, I slept and didn't sleep. Heart pounding in my throat, my wrists. I took some Advil and tried to forget what had happened but my attempt to forget produced additional remembering. I stayed close to my phone, looking at the screen again and again, until I became the thing I looked at: the reflected thing—

the face, the sharp and jutting cheekbones. I waited—hoping to feel something again, to be made to feel—for the blank screen to light up with news of the world, to illuminate itself with anything from the present.

4

I woke and texted Parker.

    Me: i need to talk
    Parker: WHAT IS IT
    Me: let's meet
    PARKER: MCDONALDS AT NINE

Parker always texted in capital letters. It was, he said, a playful rebellion against the juvenile obsession with lowercase-letter texting, which had been a rebellion against normative grammatical practices and, by extension, against normativity in its more consequential forms. He argued that, by now, lowercase texting was itself a normative practice, and should be stopped immediately. In his minor rebellion against minor rebellions, Parker claimed to want nothing—neither progress nor reaction. His was a rebellion for its own sake or, as he had put it: expression without content. An anti-anti-establishment attitude.

•

We met at the McDonald's on Shattuck Avenue. It had recently been renovated to look newer in model but older in style, so that now, instead of a 1990s cafeteria, the restaurant resembled a 1950s ski lodge—or the idea of a ski lodge, but filtered through a computer program, printed out in 3D. Pixelated imitation-pinewood panels lined the walls. The chairs were plastic but made to look like wood. The tables, too. And the bright yellows and reds of the past had been replaced with calmer greens and browns, as in a forest. The place was clean. Sterile, even. Like a hospital or a school. The light fixtures hung low from the ceiling and reflected on the tiled floor.

I stood in line. A man with a long grey beard and oversized purple sunglasses was next to me. His teeth chattered.

Noxious aromas of grease and burning cheese drifted in from behind the facade of digital kiosks where students and homeless people punched their orders onto a screen. When it was my turn, I hit the "coffee" button, and the kiosk produced a small paper cup, and filled it with coffee. This is how I avoided interfacing with the cashiers.

I sat down in the booth next to the window.

Parker had a long face and a cleft chin. He wore round bottle-cap glasses and one of those walrus mustaches—the kind that had been popular with hipsters fifteen years earlier.

He chewed his Big Mac, mouth wide open. He rested his elbow on the table and held the Big Mac with one hand and rotated it counterclockwise with the index finger and thumb, biting at the edges, and, while chewing, fixed his eyes on the sandwich, plotting his next bite.

I didn't know they sold those this early, I said.

What?

Big Macs, I said. I didn't know you could get them for breakfast.

He looked at his sandwich and shrugged.

Parker forced himself to eat at McDonald's twice a week. He would order a Big Mac with extra cheese, large fries, and a soda. He believed that Americans had a moral and ethical responsibility to eat fast food because they created it. We should suffer the consequences of the world we built, he said. You know some people can only afford to eat out at McDonald's, he said, are we better than them? Most of our peers condescended to McDonald's customers, but Parker condescended to people who refused to be McDonald's customers. When others mentioned the destructive forces of fast food (greenhouse gas emissions, excessive pollution, the obesity epidemic, blue water overuse), Parker countered with quasi-religious arguments about collective guilt, intergroup emotions, universal retribution and "the great reckoning." He believed that eating at McDonald's, or any fast-food establishment, was punishment for the excesses and decadence of late capitalism. We ought to spend our lives, Parker used to say, cultivating the death drive.

But right now, despite his masochism, he seemed to be enjoying his sandwich. He bobbed his head in sync with "Rhythm of The Night" playing from the overhead speakers.

I asked him how he was doing, and he said fine how about you and I said, Okay, I guess.

You wanted to talk.

Something happened, I said. Last night.

He was chewing.

I think someone was shot.

Someone is always getting shot, he said.

No, I mean. I think there was a shooting last night.

Parker looked up at me. His glasses magnified his eyes.

Outside, I said. Right outside my apartment. Someone was shot.

He swallowed. You watch the news too much.

I wasn't watching the news.

Okay.

Okay, what?

Nothing, he said. I just mean, it's like, you know. Welcome to where you've been. People get shot all the time here. People die.

Okay, but this was right outside my room. This is different.

Is it different? Different from what? You weren't in danger, were you? You might as well have been watching the news. What's the difference?

I took out my phone and started searching the internet for news of the previous night. There had been a fight at a dog park and petty theft near campus. I found reports about public intoxication, public urination, vandalism, indecent exposure, and prostitution. Nothing about a shooting.

Parker took another bite and started chewing and paused and said slowly, Don't turn around. Don't. Turn. Around.

I turned around.

A lanky man with long hair and thin beard dressed in a mud-colored trench coat was striding toward us, kicking his feet out and snapping them back onto the ground.

I turned back. Who is that?

Name is Josh. Hangs out here a lot. Really wild guy. Don't look at him, he'll try to talk to us.

I turned and turned back and turned again and resumed my internet search.

The man must have noticed me noticing him because now he stopped and stood over me. He looked tired.

I looked at him and looked at Parker and Parker looked at me and then looked down at the table.

The man stood there longer than felt appropriate. He stepped back and spoke to me. You know, he said, you drink too much caffeine.

What?

Yeah, he said. I can tell. Too much caffeine. Look at that coffee, man. What is that? Thirty-two ounces? Why do you do that to yourself? They're trying to kill you with that. And you wonder why you don't sleep well. And you wonder why your brain is all fucked up.

My brain?

Parker was still looking at the table, chewing.

Look, he said. They see everything you do before you do it. He pointed at my iPhone. He pointed at my coffee. Reality is a place you do not exist, he said.

Who are you?

He stepped toward me and put his hand on my shoulder. His hand was warm and heavy. He squeezed me. I am the shepherd, he said.

Parked snorted.

The shepherd, he said, and nodded and smiled kindly and walked away.

When he was going, Parker looked up again. I love these people, he said. Wackos.

Right, I said, but inwardly I felt a kind of confusion that I stupidly experienced as intimacy, as love. Did this shepherd love me?

Stupid.

Suddenly I didn't feel like drinking my coffee. I stood up and poured it out into the trashcan and brought my empty cup back to the table.

The light was moving, and the restaurant got brighter and brighter. Just then, I heard someone screaming.

Parker rolled his eyes and said again, don't look.

I looked.

The shepherd had walked over to the kiosk and was wailing wordlessly. He cranked back his neck and looked up at the fluorescent light and moaned and wailed and babbled and made speech-like sounds as if in praying or casting a spell. Now he leaned forward and threw his head and swayed and twitched like a body possessed. It was as if some angel or demon of speech had taken hold of him. The non-words pouring out of his mouth seemed almost to make sense, almost to communicate something of great importance.

Now he made his hand into the shape of a

gun. He pointed it up and down. He pointed it at his own head. Now he squatted down.

The restaurant manager came out from behind the counter and asked the man to leave. Excuse me, he cried. Sir, excuse me! He was chewing gum, and his mouth made the sound of a clicking pen. Sir, sir! I will be forced to call the police if you do not go, leave the premises immediately. Excuse me, sir. He thumbed his little mustard tie.

Now the shepherd pulled down his pants to show the lower half of his body, hairless and leather-like. He squatted deeper and deeper, closer and closer to the floor. He looked as if he was about to defecate right there, then.

The manager turned back to look at the employees standing behind the facade of kiosks. He made his hand into a phone—thumb and pinky stretched out—and put it up to his face. Call, he said. Call it in.

An employee picked up the phone and walked back into the kitchen area, out of public sight.

Josh strained and groaned and went on babbling in his demonic language.

No, he wouldn't really do it.

He would.

He was.

Doing it.

A soft blob pushed out of him and collected onto the floor—a dark embryo-like organism with red and green veins, lumpy, festering, hot.

Someone screamed and cursed. Someone gagged.

Josh pushed a final time and yelled something awful and finished and pulled up his pants and walked casually out the door.

The manager ran behind the counter and came back with gloves and cleaning supplies and immediately started cleaning up the mess. He turned his head away from it even as he tried to wipe it clean. He sprayed and wiped and wiped and sprayed again and went on muttering repeatedly to himself, it's okay, it's okay, it's okay.

The place was clearing out, almost empty now.

What was I doing? I was thinking about the prophet. Ezekiel. I was thinking about bread. You could make bread out of that shit, I thought. You could eat it.

•

Parker hadn't once looked up from his food. He took another bite of his burger and smacked his lips and chewed.

Didn't you see that?

It's just shit.

I don't think I can sit here anymore.

Parker shrugged.

I have a headache.

Another one? You need to see a therapist. I know a good one, young guy. He's helped me a lot. Everyone needs to see a therapist. Everyone is sick.

Okay.

I'm texting you the number right now.

I drank from my empty cup.

Parker finished eating and crumpled his Big Mac wrapper into a ball and set it on his tray. How's your writing? he said. How's that going?

I wanted to tell him that I hadn't worked on my novel in over a year, that I was on the verge of giving up writing altogether, that I was and wasn't a writer. But I didn't. We had established our friendship on writing fiction, and I didn't want to jeopardize the only real friendship I had in Berkeley.

Fine, I said. Great.

Great, he said. When can I read it?

When I'm done.

A silence hung over us for several minutes and I looked down into my cup and saw a dark excrement stain of coffee in the shape of a fish.

Now the police arrived. Four, five, six of them paced around the restaurant looking at the customers. They wore dark glasses and helmets. They tucked their hands into their black leather duty belts. One of them stood next to our table. I couldn't see the eyes behind his sunglasses, couldn't tell where he was looking.

Dude, Parker said. I think you need to make some friends. I think that's your problem.

I didn't know I had a problem.

You've been here almost six months and you have no new friends.

I drank from the empty cup again.

Come to a party tonight.

Whose party?

You don't know her.

I'm not going to a party if I'm not invited.

Everyone's invited, he said. I'm going to pick you up.

I don't know.

Nine, he said. Pick you up at nine.

5

I stuffed an empty flask and a pack of cigarettes in my pocket and waited outside. Before long, Parker pulled up in his maroon Nissan Altima and rolled down the window and gestured towards the front seat. I got in. Three people were crammed into the back. Parker introduced them. Julio, Leea, and Khushal. I said my name and waved into the back seat.

Hi. Hello.

Screens lit up their faces.

Parker wore a pink and purple vintage '80s style windbreaker that made him look anachronistically relevant, whereas I was now wearing a loose grey cardigan, characterless and frayed and snagged along the chest and back with a hole in the elbow, which I thought I could get away with because the beige elbow patch happened to be the same color as my skin.

I had apparently killed the conversation when I got into the car because, as soon as I shut my door, Julio started talking in an annoyed kind of way. Anyway, he said, like I said, we don't have very many options. Politically, you know. They force us into camps.

I watched the backseat in the rearview mirror, occasionally turning my head to nod and let them know I was listening.

That's right, Parker said. I'm an old school Marxist, which means I don't exist anymore.

And I'm a Nihilistic Futurist, Julio said. So, I don't exist yet.

Khushal and Leea held in unison a sustained hmm sound to indicate either recognition or approval.

Julio tapped me on the shoulder. What about you?

Me?

What are you?

Me? Nothing.

What do you do?

I work for a startup.

Right.

I make content.

Oh.

And emails.

He's a writer, said Parker.

A writer, Julio repeated.

He's writing a novel, said Parker.

A novel.

A novel.

About what?

I remembered Zeke. It's about a thirty something, I said, living in Berkeley writing a novel about a thirty something living in Berkeley.

No one laughed.

Gross, said Julio.

Not really, though, I said. It's about—I made something up—a clown.

Khushal googled "clown novels" and told me how many other novels about clowns already existed: *It* by Steven King, *The Clown* by Heinrich Böll, *Shalimar the Clown* by Salman Rushdie, *Clown*

Girl by Monica Drake, *Sacred Clowns* by Tony Hillerman, *City of Clowns* by Daniel Alarcón.

Leea, still on her phone, said, what does your clown represent?

I hate that word, Parker said. *Represent.*

Tell us about it, said Leea, your novel.

Give us the whole thing, Julio said.

I hesitated.

Go on.

The whole thing.

Okay. I gave them a summary, something long. I spoke nervously, frantically even, but I liked telling stories more than I liked talking about myself, so I went all in. I said as much as I could. Whenever I paused or tried to stop the story, someone—usually Parker or Julio—pushed me to keep going, to finish. It went like this:

He'd rather not be a clown, but he makes people laugh. He makes them afraid, too. He wonders why. Why are they laughing? Why are they afraid? His life goes on. He believes in God, gets lonely, smokes cigarettes, drinks in the morning. Masturbates a lot—that type of thing. Certain people love him because he's so sad. He's so sad that he's funny. They find him whimsical and amusing, but really, he's on the verge of losing his mind. He wears orange pants and bright t-shirts. He wears loafers without socks. He spends a lot of time writing in his journal. He performs at birthday parties and in local events. But the art of clowning is dead, he thinks. Clowns are more irrelevant than ever. Not only irrelevant but disagreeable. They have taken a new, unlikable form.

He thinks I should have been a lawyer, a banker, a politician. Soon he discovers like-minded folks on the internet with whom he shares his experiences, his feelings—entire digital spaces full of male clowns. There, he finds purpose and meaning. At first, he spends, I don't know, maybe an hour or two online every day, but as the days pass, he finds his virtual interactions increasingly stimulating. He spends more and more time online. His digital life is more fulfilling and rewarding than his real one. He begins to think there is no difference between them, that there should be no difference. There is no such thing as "one true reality." Eventually, he spends most of his days on the internet—his eyes fixate and reflect the rapidly changing lights on the screen, his mouth droops open, exhaling shortened breath. His hands tremble as they type to keep up with the speed of internet thought. He joins a group called "Clowns Against Non-clowns," where he engages in anti-anti-clown rhetoric. He participates in all manner of online shenanigans: trolling, meme-making, etc. He quits his job as a clown to become an artist, a pioneer of the new digital "clown aesthetic." He buys a fancy camera and starts to make internet performance art. Overnight he achieves fame for a YouTube video in which he stages his suicide. This is where he finally fulfills his clown potential. That's what he tells himself. He makes several films, several suicides. After each performance, of course, he kills himself. In the first video, he shoots himself in the head. In the second video, he hangs himself. As you'd guess, the scene is highly offensive and controversial. It looks authentic. The first time he does this, the video goes viral within a few hours. Of course, thousands of people report the video, and YouTube removes it. The clown—supported by his online community of clowns and emboldened by his newfound internet attention—issues a statement of artistic intent, which he publishes on Twitter. The reactions to his performance art are mixed. Internet art critics praise the work. Some call it "a brave realization of the logical conclusion of toxic masculinity." One critic writes, "his work implicates the community in the act of individual suicide, the viewer is forced to witness the death of the other and recognize his culpability therein." Casual observers of his videos find them distasteful and offensive. One blogger calls him "an angsty and melodramatic adolescent man, another crisis of masculinity." Still, another critic says that his art lacks any real political power, "it can only shock and unsettle but cannot change anyone's mind." One person writes in the comments: "The intent of the artist is too vague for this to be anything other than trolling." Another person agrees: "Because there is no systemic critique here, we have no choice but to read this as an act of aggression." Because his videos incite controversy and anger, I said, YouTube continues to take them off their website. Later, YouTube deletes the clown's account and bans him from using the site altogether. He protests this decision. He writes several letters and emails to YouTube arguing his case. He never receives a reply. No one contacts him. He cannot infiltrate the bureaucratic fortresses of internet capitalism. He launches a website where he can post videos freely. He doesn't have as much traffic at first, but he garners enough attention that he can sell advertisements to make a living. "The clown who kills himself." He performs all types of suicides: gas, poison, prescription drugs, heroin, freezing, jumping in front of a train, asphyxiation, drowning, starvation, self-immolation, even hari-kari. Each time looks as real as the time before. Once, he almost accidentally kills himself. He feels exhilarated. Transcendent. He can't ever fully replicate the experience, though he tries. More and more he wants to approximate death as carefully as he can. This becomes a kind of addiction. Some commentators say, "He's challenging the very nature of reality." Others say, "He's inviting us to think about death as an art form and therefore as a kind of fiction." When he runs out of ideas, he decides, against his better judgement, to reenact the suicides of famous men: Kurt Cobain, Mark Rothko, Paul Celan, Robert Oppenheimer, Ernest Hemingway, Hunter S. Thompson, Vladimir Mayakovsky, Vincent van Gogh, David Foster Wallace, Robin Williams, Walter Benjamin, and so on. Here, he goes too far. The clown's critics begin to attack him for "theft." They accuse him of representing experiences that don't belong to him. His more sophisticated opponents call him an appropriationist. His more pedestrian commentators refer to him as "a sellout," "out of touch." Meanwhile, elsewhere, some social documentary students, eager for a story, decide to make a full-feature documentary about the clown. And the clown, now concerned for the future of his reputation and, by extension, his career and livelihood, agrees to participate. The cameras arrive at his home three weeks later. The following interview takes place:

Interviewer: Did you expect this level of backlash?

Clown: Backlash?

Interviewer: Regarding your suicide reenactments.

Clown: I was doing what I'd always been doing: killing myself over and over in a variety of ways and with a variety of tools. I think some people are upset because they don't understand my method. But that's what art is. It's a trick. It's a magic show.

A year or later, when the documentary finally comes out, the clown is devastated by what he sees. The documentarians paint him as a lonely, desolate, self-hating figure whose suicide performances are merely testing ground for fantasies of self- annihilation. In response, the clown announces that he will retire after one final performance, in which he will complete an actual suicide. The event is to take place in real time, on a live webcam. He's going to kill himself, this time for real. But before he does, he receives hundreds of letters encouraging him to complete the killing. Kill yourself for real this time you piece of shit. I hope you slit your wrists so I can watch you bleed to death. But he also receives kind emails from current and former fans imploring him to stay alive.

You have brought awareness to a world blind to the endemic of suicide. You are a hero. These letters cause him to weep, though he does not know whether he weeps for them or himself. On the day of the event, the clown sets up his computer and delivers his final speech. When it's time for him to kill himself, he stands up, drinks a glass of water, and walks out of the room. He does not return. The webcam continues to run. The world—or the small portion of it that happens to be interested in experimental internet performance art—watches for hours. Nothing happens. The camera continues to run. It shows only the clown's dull living room: a leather couch, torn on the armrest where he used to put his feet, above which hung a print. The webcam runs for days. People continue to watch—watching nothing, waiting for something to happen. And this is how the story ends. The clown never comes back into the room. Some of his viewers call the police, but no one knows his address. When the police eventually locate him, he isn't there. He isn't there, but he isn't anywhere else either.

Parker was nodding in approval, though probably ironically.

Julio went, Ah. Ah, I see. It's one of those sly literary books, all Starbucks-like, that leaves you feeling cold and headless. Something to meditate.

Khushal: I thought the existential novel died in the 70s.

Leea: So, does he kill himself?

Khushal: A metaphor for the failure of metaphor.

Leea: An allegory of oppression, maybe.

Khushal: So, the oppressed are represented in the form of a clown?

Parker: The problem is that the very concept of a clown is relative to the hierarchies of the dominant culture. What is a clown even, and to whom is he clowning?

Julio: It sounds like it's about white supremacy.

I leaned my head against the window, trying to distance myself physically from the conversation.

Leea: Can't he just be a clown?

Khushal: Wait, okay. Is he oppressed or is he a Nazi?

He's a Fascist, said Julio.

As the conversation went on, I became unable to tell who was kidding, who wasn't. I pressed my head harder into the glass. A sitcom-feeling of imbecility overcame me.

Parker: Is it even possible for someone to know the difference between good and evil?

No, said Julio, the clown is a representative of fascists. That's how I read him. He's a white supremacist at least. Sad little man. I think you should change the ending of the novel. Make the clown kill himself.

Leea: Every clown is a fascist?

Julio: Have you heard of Clown World? It's one of those memes on 4chan and Reddit. They say that Leftist politics are clown politics, leftist media are clown media. So, the fascists appropriated a new symbol for themselves. The Clown.

Like Pepe. Like the OK sign and the Boogaloo. Maybe he is a Boogaloo?

Khushal: Myth of the down-and-out white.

Leea: Don't assume he's white.

Julio: He is.

Leea: Is he?

Julio: Isn't he?

Khushal: Why wouldn't he be?

Julio (to me): Aren't you white?

Me: Me?

Julio: I can't tell.

Khushal (laughing): How white are you?

Me: I'm Sephardic. Kind of.

Julio: Kind of Jewish?

Me: Half Jewish. Turkish.

Julio: So, you're white.

Khushal: Very white.

Julio: Clown.

I felt a shame so crippling that shame was not the word for it. The world went blurry—a metaphor of fog becoming a literal inability to see. I tasted my own tongue. Something bitter, metallic. I looked at my broken wristwatch.

Wait, Parker interrupted, but, if the real world is a clown world, then is the clown a symbol of fascism, or its enemies? Wouldn't the mainstream politician be a type of clown in the world of clown politics? Or is fascism dressing itself up in clown paint and masks to mock the 'clown world' they disavow? Who exactly is the clown in this symbolic order?

I don't think there's any order in what the fascists do, Julio said. It's chaos they want. There are also rumors that they're trying to co-opt the rainbow and the thumbs up, too. And for no other reason than to cause chaos, so that no one knows what's real and what's fake.

•

We arrived at the party. People everywhere. Parker double parked the car in the driveway, and we walked around the back of the house and entered through a rusted metal gate that led into the backyard.

The house was nothing to speak of—a small one-story red brick home, with small round windows, and the backyard was all weeds and dirt, enclosed by a short concrete wall.

Want to smoke before we go in? Parker reached into his shirt pocket and pulled out three pre-rolled joints.

The patio had a picnic table and a few lawn chairs and a makeshift fire pit—a semicircle of stones where a pile of coals crackled.

I sat in a beach chair next to Parker. Khushal gathered twigs beneath the trees, and threw them one by one onto the coals, where they instantly ignited.

The house shook from the crowd noise, the music. People circulated in and out through the screen door, which swung open and closed and each time smacked against the doorframe. I wondered whether Ezekiel was inside. I looked at the house. I scanned the backyard, trying to find him—wanting and not wanting to see him.

Parker lit the joint and took a long hit and blew and passed it to me. I sucked and sucked again and held the smoke in my mouth, careful not to inhale, and pretended to gulp, to swallow, and turned my head to the side and blew it out. I handed the joint to Leea, and she pressed her lips down and inhaled once, twice. She crossed and uncrossed her legs.

Julio took a hit. Do we really need another novel with a disaffected male narrator?

He's not disaffected, said Leea, looking at me. He's just awkward.

Khushal—his hands were trembling—took one hit and turned to face me and blew out. Why don't we just ask our author what he means? What does the clown mean? Who is he really?

He's just an artist, I don't know.

They laughed, almost in unison. Their eyes became increasingly small and red as they passed the joint around.

Please no more novels about artists, Julio said. No more art. No more religion. No more quote-unquote weird sex. No more violence.

Our conversation ended when another group entered through the same gate and approached and greeted us. Everyone knew everyone else except for me. They hugged and kissed or didn't hug or kiss but shook hands or nodded hello. The new group was Omar, Henry, Jackie, and Janice. Parker introduced me as "the clown writer," and I nodded to downplay my embarrassment. I took the empty flask out of my pocket and pretended to drink to discourage anyone from asking me about my "clown" writing, which they didn't.

For a long time, there was lively discussion and arguments about this and that—guns, gender, the future of art, freedom, social media, post-woke-ism, whether white guilt was another version of white privilege, whether white allyship was part of the white savior complex. The whole time, I did what anyone would do. I shut my mouth is what I did. I shrunk down, made myself invisible.

Soon the weed was smoked, and the air looked thick and painted with palpable, impasto brushstrokes—the kind that causes a painting's subject matter to stick out from the canvas.

As the smoke began to dissipate, Parker stood up and the two groups headed off toward the house. I stayed in my seat and held up my flask and said to no one in particular, I'm going to stay out here for a while. I want to finish this off.

No one seemed to care.

My plan, in truth, was to sit there for a few minutes, and eventually order an Uber back to Berkeley.

Soon everyone was gone except for Janice. She looked at me and made a face that I would come to recognize as distinctly her own.

I'll join you, she said. If that's cool.

She sat down and turned, and the light ran down her face. For the first time, I could see her clearly. She had a young, athletic body, thin but muscular, but she wore an old woman's face—her mouth sagged at the edges, always almost frowning.

The coals and twigs popped and cracked and I thought about the gunshots from the previous night. I thought to ask Janice about it, but thought better.

She pointed to my flask. You going to share that?

I held the flask up with two fingers and shook it out. Sorry, I said. That was the last of it.

Janice scowled and stood and headed for the house. Wait here, she said.

While she was gone, I found a stack of logs on the side of the house and took one and set it on top of the coals to keep the fire going and went back to get a second log but felt suddenly ridiculous—why was I tending to this fire?—and sat down.

Janice returned, breathing hard. She held up to show me an open bottle of wine. I stole it, she said. We can share.

Red wine gives me headaches.

Janice put her lips around the mouth of the bottle and threw back her head and gulped. She extended the bottle toward me, and, despite my initial rejection, I accepted, and drank.

We were silent for a long time, watching the flame twist and turn and cast circles around us. I felt myself wanting to say something. To break the silence. So, I blurted out a boring question and followed it up with stupid question and another boring question. How do you know Parker? I said. Do you work together? What do you do for work?

She shook her head. No.

No?

No.

No, you don't work?

Work, she said. Of course, I work. Work is whatever. I don't want to talk about work. I don't want to make small talk. It's so dull, you know. It's so boring *small* talking with someone you might never see again. What if we never see each other after tonight? We will have wasted a whole night talking about—what? Work? Where you were born, and what your hobbies are, and where you went to school. Why should I care about all that if I don't even know you?

I hummed.

We've got the getting-to-know-people thing backward, she said. We meet people in all the wrong ways. The wrong order. The first thing you should know about someone is their political and religious beliefs. Maybe their greatest fear, biggest regret, most embarrassing story. That kind of thing.

Okay, I said. Tell me one. An embarrassing story.

Nothing embarrasses me, she said. Shame is boring.

Oh. I put my mouth on the bottle and drank. Okay, I said, not embarrassing then. Tell me anything.

She leaned back and seemed to think. Okay, she said. I have one.

Go ahead.

48

A few years ago, I started dating this guy. Total airhead. Good body though. A gym rat, whatever you'd call it. We went on three dates, and I was into him, but not that into him. After dinner, we agreed that we'd fulfilled our dating requirements and that it was time to move to the next phase of our relationship. We agreed to have sex the next night. So, the next day, he comes over to my apartment, comes in the door, and he's waddling all duck-like. He asks to use the bathroom and tells me that he needs a plastic bag. I give him a trash bag and point him in the direction of the bathroom. He's in there for like, I don't know, twenty minutes. He takes a shower. It's quiet for a long time. When he comes out, trash bag in hand, he tells me that he sharted himself, and had to walk four blocks with poop running down his leg. What? I say. Sharted, he says. What? He explained that he needed a trash bag for his underwear, and he kept saying sorry, I'm sorry, he says I'm sorry, I thought it was just a fart, and I'm like, dude, super grossed out at this point, but I'm trying to be open-minded. And he had just taken a shower and so—

You fucked him anyway?

—I fucked him anyway.

No way.

Just then, right on cue, Janice's phone started ringing: a circus theme. She removed it from her pocket. Sorry, sorry. I need to take it. Hold on. She stood and walked and opened the backyard gate and went away.

I looked at my phone, though there was

nothing there to see. My background image was a stock photograph of sand dunes at night—a barren desert landscape under a full moon.

I kept looking and eventually it vibrated. *Three friends massacred on fishing trip; manhunt underway. Pair of 'dangerous' fugitives who escaped Virginia jail may be in Pennsylvania, officials say. Woman fatally shot in NYC after asking man to stop setting off fireworks. Portland police declare 'riot' after fires set, fences moved.*

Janice returned and sat down.

Crazy story, I said. Incredible.

She put her hand on my knee and leaned in. It's not over yet, she said. So, we're doing it and, you know, I'm on top and looking down at the dude, and suddenly he starts screaming no. I'm like, should I stop? And he says no. So I keep going, but he keeps yelling no. Like, no. No! Loud, too. Like, scary loud. And I'm freaking out because I'm riding him and he's yelling no, but he doesn't want me to stop. And then his face gets all distorted, and his mouth slips, all sagging and drooping to the side like a Picasso painting. And then he starts coming, and he's screaming, and then, not kidding, he starts to shit. He's shitting and coming at the same time, and it's warm and thick and wet. And it's everywhere. It keeps coming and coming. But this is the weirdest part, she said. As soon as he starts shitting, I start coming, too. I can't explain it. I don't know. I didn't feel myself approaching climax until that point, but somehow, we had achieved that ideal situation where you and your partner both come at the same time, but as I'm having this totally awesome orgasm, I'm also, you know, covered in shit. And I can smell the shit. I can feel it all over me. But there's nothing I can do. It's like a horror movie and a religious experience at the same time.

I can't believe it. I don't.

It's true, she said. I had to get an entirely new mattress, bed sheets, everything. That guy was so embarrassed he didn't even stay to help me clean up. He Venmoed me more than enough money for a new mattress, bed frame, sheets. So, I did get an upgrade out of the whole thing, at least. But it felt weird like he had paid me money to take a shit in my bed. I felt like a sex worker. A sex worker of twisted shit fantasies. I never heard from him again.

I can't believe it, I said again, but in a slightly louder voice this time, to let her know that I sincerely couldn't believe it and wasn't merely adhering to the niceties of conversation.

The light was directly above her head, and it set a silver-purple glow across her hair, and, for a moment, she looked like a completely different person, someone familiar, someone I had known.

Which was more unbelievable: the story, or the fact that she told it? Why had she told it? Was she trying to communicate something indirectly, some sexual preference? Some erotic deviancy? Did she hope that I would infer some coded meaning? It didn't matter. The story caused me to feel instantly and inexplicably close to her. She seemed to become a longtime friend, a potential lover, and, like an idiot, I wondered whether I was falling in love with her, and that feeling felt wrong, and that's why it felt good. We had an instant bond, something deeper and more vulnerable than mutual life circumstances. And I recognized something in her I lacked. A casual buoyancy. An openness. I wanted that.

6

We shared an Uber. When the driver dropped me off at my house, Janice stepped out of the car and walked in with me and told him that she was getting out here. Neither of us said anything about it, and it felt more exciting that way, each of us intuitively wanting the same thing without having to articulate it.

Opening the door, I could hear my housemates laughing in the kitchen, rowdy, the whole group of them. I grabbed Janice's elbow and led her to my room and closed the door.

When I flipped the light on, Janice covered her eyes with her hair to shield them and made a joke about being a vampire. For a few seconds, she paced the room as if unsure where to place herself. She stumbled and slurred her words. She looked at her phone and laughed at nothing, something on her private screen. She looked at my bookshelf and fingered the books, tracing the spines of each.

Do you really read them?

I used to.

Expensive wallpaper, she said and mumbled something I couldn't understand.

It was then that I realized I had a problem. Janice was drunk. Too drunk. And I suddenly didn't feel comfortable being around her.

Now she reached into her pocket and took out a piece of gum and put it in her mouth and violently chewed, forcefully breathing through her nose so that she seemed to be laughing. She threw the wrapper into the trashcan.

Hey, she said, pointing down. Why are you throwing *this* away?

Throwing what away?

Why are you throwing this away? She reached into the trashcan and took out the tote I had thrown away the previous night. (I had forgotten it was there.) This, she said, lifting the bag and looking it over. She held it up to me and smiled. Are you into this?

Am I what?

Are you into this?

This?

She pointed at the arrows. *This, this. this.*

Before I had time to think I said, Yes. Yes, I said. Yes, I am.

After looking me over for a while and sustaining a meditative look—head back and he chin up—she said, Me, too.

You, too?

She seemed pleased. She grinned. Yeah, she said. Yes. I am.

I thought to ask her if she knew Ezekiel but didn't.

After a while, she sat down at the head of the bed and looked me up and down. After a long pause, she lifted her skirt in a joking way and slurred her vowels as she spoke. If you want to have sex, I think she said, that's okay with me. But it's going to be lazy.

I sat on the bed at a distance. I could feel the

heat of her body, her skin. Lazy sex. I knew what she meant, and, I admit, I did consider it. But no. She's too drunk.

No, I said aloud, afraid that I might say yes.

Come on. I'm telling you it's okay.

I looked away and down at my phone.

Whatever. Fine. Let's go to sleep. She stood up and spit out her gum and threw her body upside-down onto the bed—so that her feet lay on the headrest—and made snow angels in the sheet and undid her ponytail and let her long black hair fall across her shoulders. Her arm hung off the side so that her hand swung loosely down.

I pulled her feet up toward the top of the bed, straightened out her body, and lifted her head to place a pillow beneath it. With an old quilt I kept in the closet, I wrapped her up, and instantly—almost instantly—she closed her eyes and was asleep, still fully clothed.

I clicked off the light and watched her for a moment to make sure she was in fact sleeping. She drew breath forcefully, almost sucking it in.

For hours I lay awake, looking up at the ceiling and out the window, consumed by a particular kind of loneliness—the kind you feel when lying so close to a stranger. And I was worrying about my lie. Why had I done it? What was Janice going to expect of me now that she thought I was part of Antifa?

The lie, I thought, doesn't have to be a lie.

7

The house was quiet—Janice was still sleeping—and it seemed late enough that I could safely leave my room without risk of being seen. I stumbled down the hallway into the shared bathroom and turned on the shower and locked the door. The moonlight streamed through the small bathroom window like a spotlight illuminating a stage.

I was sitting on the toilet, waiting for the water to heat up, when the phone vibrated. *Toxic algae close beaches. Earthquakes rattle southern California. Iran sends warning to the west. Disney star dies. There's a growing call in the US to defund police as a solution to police brutality. Here's what that means.*

I clicked the icon, which took me to another icon, and another and so on—and soon I was lost in clickbait. I caught an article at the bottom of the article I was halfway reading, titled, *You Won't Believe These Celebrity Bodies.*

Would I believe them?

I clicked.

The third body photograph was a normatively beautiful celebrity whose mediocre acting career had recently imploded following a sequence of ugly scandals—sex tapes, ambiguous and therefore offensive tweets. In the photo, she walked out of the ocean. The classic Sports Illustrated Swimsuit Edition cover shot. Everything was wet. Everything expressed wetness. Her hair lay thin and plastered to one side of her face and her body was swollen. The nipples, indistinguishable from the rest of the torso, slipped out of her bikini, and the legs sagged and pulsed with thick veins and her neck and shoulders were damaged with sunspots. There was something horrible in the image. She was laughing, but in a conspiratorial kind of way. It made her look evil.

It was not the woman herself that caused blood to rush to my crotch, but the idea of the woman. She seemed real, or almost real. Present and authentic. Her body was nothing exceptional. She could be like someone I knew, had known, or would know. Someone I might meet at a bar—desiring and desperate as I was for intimacy and maybe love.

I closed my eyes the better to see, and let a short fantasy play out in my mind, as if on a screen. The whole scene, every obscene detail, was a rerun of something I'd seen before. Someone else's fantasy. Sex on the dining room table. The man was another man, and I was made to watch him. *Ezekiel. Ezekiel.* (The name came into my head.) They had generic sex, Ezekiel and the woman, in a sequence of conventional positions. Nothing deviant, nothing creative, really. Bent over, missionary, reverse cowgirl, cowgirl, reach around. He mounted, he leaned. She grabbed him by the throat and his face went colorless. Look. He was losing his composure now, stretching out his toes.

When it was finished, I turned off the bathroom light because I didn't want to see myself.

But the moonlight was still there, all over me. Like sticky milk. I looked at my broken wristwatch.

I wadded together a handful of toilet paper and held it beneath the running faucet and rubbed myself with it, still swollen with residual blood flow, plump, sticky with discharge. And I was careful when I rubbed it all clean, reverent but mildly disgusted, the way, I imagined, the Apostles washed the feet of Christ.

8

A bad energy woke me, and I found Janice already awake, still in bed, but turned away from me. She squirmed and sat up and hunched. She was looking at her phone. A video played. The volume was low, droning some monotonous, some tedious loop.

How long have you been awake?

She didn't answer.

I cleared my throat.

The protests, she said. It's all over the news. Three people died last night. Something to do with the election.

My head was killing me—the red wine.

Lots of people are worried, she said.

Where?

Everywhere.

No, I said. Where was the riot?

Not a riot, she said. A *protest*.

I got out of bed and opened the curtains. The sun was not in its place. It was late, later than I thought it should be. Children were laughing or screaming nearby.

Janice got out of bed and tried to open the window. She struggled and, when the window wouldn't budge, gave up trying and sat back down on the edge of the bed and pulled out her phone and went back to the videos. This is bad, she said.

Yeah, I said.

Silence.

Want some coffee?

People are dying out there, she said.

I didn't know if that was supposed to be an answer or whether she hadn't heard me, so I asked the question again, and again she did not answer. She held her phone up for me to see. See? she said. Watch.

I tried, but the images were unwatchable. The screen displayed a mash of limbs and faces, a clash of bodies, bodies indistinguishable from one another, moving, being moved, right and left, forward and back, undifferentiated from movement itself. It was impossible to see who was who, who was doing what, and to whom it was being done. The screen was a blur of violence and struggle, happening too fast to be properly filmed.

That's terrible, I said.

I know, she said. I know.

I went to make coffee, slow as I could—took the Brita Pitcher from the mini-fridge, poured the water into a glass, poured the glass into the coffee maker reservoir, and repeated the process until the water level hit the maximum line. I lifted the lid, rinsed the filter basket with the already-filtered Brita water over a large bowl on top of the fridge, removed an eco-friendly paper filter from its cardboard box, placed it into the filter basket, opened the drawer where I kept my coffee tin, peeled back the lid: no coffee.

So, I said. I'm out of coffee. Let's go get an americano, or what do you like?

I'm going to head home. I need to be alone.

Right. Okay.

She ordered a car and sat there for a while on the edge of my bed. She had turned up the volume, and I could hear the riots booming from the tiny machine. She watched it over and over, the same video. Explosions, flare guns, tear gas grenades, yelling.

I joined her, took out my phone and looked for something to look for on the internet.

When the car arrived, Janice beelined out, and I went with her. Should I hug her? Should I make plans to see her again?

Her head was down.

I said goodbye, but the violence continued in the background. People were still screaming on the machine. You shot him, someone yelled. You killed him.

9

A clock was ticking. Something moved. Something passed by. Almost noon. Afternoon. Evening. Janice was gone and I was sitting—still sitting—at my desk, trying to write. Something something. Nothing coming. I thought about Janice—couldn't stop thinking. The window and the light in the window moved. It felt like I was being moved. And it was then I heard—if that's the right word for it—a sound, almost a voice, an imperative, commanding me something: out, out, out. So, I got up and went, having nowhere to go and nowhere to be.

I headed north on Shattuck toward Hearst, cutting east along the north edge of the university, then dropping down, southward along Sather toward the southern entrance that connected to Telegraph, where I turned right, down Bancroft, back the way I came—west, then farther south again, then east, then west again.

The power lines hummed.

It was not yet noon and the temperature had already hit one hundred plus degrees. The sun exerted a sameness that blurred the lines between things, this and that—weeds and grass, grass and dirt, dirt and concrete, concrete and glass.

The phone went: *Drug-resistant malaria, Venezuela blackout. A glacier memorial. How Equifax exposed the personal data of millions of Americans. How Google sold face recognition software to the Chinese*

Government. So many intense emotions surround a body that is trying to die. Here's what one doctor wants patients to know about the end.

The university was out of my way, but I liked to walk there—to be seen walking. I walked among them—students and professors, almost one of them, all of them dressed in natural fibers, recycled materials, earth tones: V-neck jumpers and overalls, flannel cutoffs and denim jackets, wool hats and army boots, infinity scarves and faded ripped jeans, beige shoulder bags and Swedish backpacks.

By the time I noticed the protest on campus, it was too late to avoid the crowd and I couldn't just turn around and walk the other direction. Not now.

Almost all protests in Berkeley started or ended at Sather Gate. The gate—made of bronze and steel metalwork—had long ago been named a Historic Landmark, listed on the National Register of Historic Places as an established icon of the anti-establishment. Something was always being protested at Sather—the living wage, tuition increases, international relations, police brutality, workers' rights. And so I recognized the present scene. The SA, SU, US, UTA, ASUC, BAMN, LBM, BSA, AAS, AAC, ESLP, and SEC were there with clipboards and leaflets, chapbooks and pamphlets. Pop, Rap, and Pop Rap played too loudly on some unseen speakers, giving the gathering a celebratory quality, an expression of joy in dissonance. Students, tech-types, artists, and lifelong activists clustered around the gate, picketing and chanting and singing and clapping their hands and marching in circles. They took photos and videos to post on the internet. Antifa was there, too, with its satellite groups, clad in Ninja uniforms: black bandanas, tight black pants, hoods, scarves, ski masks.

Was Zeke among them, the anonymous? Was Janice? Should I have been over there with them?

I took my phone and put in my headphones and pretended to receive a call. I was like, Hello? and stopped walking. Yes, I said, I'll be there, and continued walking. Of course. That's what they're saying, I said. Unbelievable. Watermelon, watermelon. Yes. Okay. Good, good. No problem. See you soon.

One protester noticed me and—determined to enforce my participation—shoved a flier in front of my face while walking stride for stride beside me. He shouted something I couldn't hear. I took the flyer and nodded without making eye contact. The protestor shouted something, something else. I forced a smile, making sure to show my teeth. But immediately I worried that my smile might reflect the physical discomfort I was feeling—that it looked more like a scowl than a smile, and I worried the protestor might think I was grimacing at him and his cause, and so, to counteract my grimace, I made a new face: eyebrow furrowed, mouth turned down.

The protester waved his hand, pointing and drawing shapes or letters in the air. He slapped the palm of one hand with the backhand of another. He pointed up at the sky and down at the ground. And I became aware of the possibility that even my contemplative face looked like something else, that what I hoped would communicate thoughtfulness, expressed its opposite— impatience, anger. Now I made an array of faces, moving all my features, never settling on a single expression.

He yelled something and moved toward another passerby.

The phone vibrated again. *California State health officials are investigating a virus outbreak at a nursing facility near San Francisco. U.S. stocks are heading toward their worst week in 12 years and investors want to know where it will all end. Iran's nuclear program. Three dead in Texas explosion. Protesters have been grabbed off the street by federal police in camouflage and body armor and forced into unmarked vans.*

I pressed forward, head down. My shirt clung to my skin. I opened all my social media apps, and indiscriminately "liked" every single photograph, every post, every political rant, every joke, every shared link that I could find.

Far away now and alone, I sat down on a bench and looked at my broken wristwatch. I went into my texts and found the number for Parker's therapist. I called and made an appointment.

We can wedge you in tomorrow, said the voice in my ear.

Tomorrow is good.

As soon as I hung up, the phone went:

Multiple dead in a bombing of a shopping center in Florida. A state of emergency has been declared in Southern California as the region continues to experience aftereffects of multiple earthquakes. Cockroaches are developing cross-resistance to insecticides that can be passed on to their offspring.

I clicked on the icon and watched, half-watching, videos online: a political speech by the Presidential Candidate K, and a satirical impersonation of Candidate K on a late-night TV show. I watched a lecture on the death of religion, a talk on the rebirth of religion, a controversial performance from a famous stand-up comic about masturbating in public, a lecture on the various iterations of Stalinism in Hollywood films, a lecture on the use of archetypes in political narratives. I saw a kid chugging a gallon of milk, high school cheerleaders eating ghost peppers, cats playing ping pong, high school baseball players putting pepperoni on their nipples and streaking around their neighborhood, Mormon missionaries snorting cocaine off a coffee table. I saw a Philadelphia Eagles fan covering himself—in Dionysian ecstasy—in horse shit; a French soccer player simulating oral sex on a raw chicken, a tech mogul trying to have sex with a whale, a website called *the nicest place on the internet,* where, for a small fee—I paid it—I saw random people waving and smiling and pretending to hug me through the screen and complimenting my clothes, my teeth, my cheekbones.

And suddenly, in real life, I saw it. Blood. My hand was covered in it—a wet crimson streak that ran from the top of my middle finger to the base of my palm. I tried to wipe it off with my other hand, but only smeared it around, spreading it widthwise across my wrists and forearms. Now it was on both hands. Now I was panicking, and my panic occurred to me as an allusion to something else, and therefore of a cliché. Bloody hands. I looked around to find anyone to ask: Do you see this?

Now I bent and licked my hands frantically to clean them and my tongue stiffened at the taste of sulfur and salt. I looked around again and examined my whole body.

Oh. I found it.

Without noticing, and for an unknown length of time, I had been scratching at the back of my calf. A mosquito bite. I'd been scratching the bite so hard that I'd cut myself, tore away a piece of my own flesh the size of a dime. But because I had scratched so thoughtlessly, so intensely but without intent, it would be inaccurate to say that I, this me, had done it at all. It had been done to me. Was done. Blood ran from the cut down my leg and onto my foot.

The wind must have been blowing, though it was not the wind I noticed, but my body noticing the wind. I was shivering, and the hairs on my arms and neck went upright. The day was clear, but the wind—if wind it was—suggested a shift in weather pattern. Oncoming rain, or worse.

10

Next day, late afternoon, I walked to my appointment. The first of seven prepaid meetings with the therapist.

His office was located on the top floor of a concrete building and it had a window that overlooked other concrete buildings, with windows identical to themselves, and against which the late-morning sun hit directly, so that each long sheet of glass functioned more like a mirror than a window.

The office itself was narrow and bare. It had one desk, one yellow rug, one glass table, and one bookshelf. It had two large chairs, which faced one sofa—the same chair, but twice, i.e., two of one chair—crimson, leather armchair with chrome dragon feet.

The therapist was pacing from desk to window to bookshelf and back to desk, as if looking for something to look for. He had one hand in his pocket and the other on the back of his neck.

He pointed at the sofa and told me to have a seat.

The sofa smelled new but looked old. A false antique, flame mahogany, with carved cornucopia knobs at the knees, upholstered with a pink floral pattern, tufted with enormous buttons.

I sat down. I looked at my broken wristwatch.

The air conditioner blew a colder-than-necessary breeze directly above me, causing my hair to flap repeatedly against my forehead.

The therapist opened the drawer and produced a brown file folder, packed with multicolored sheets of paper. He sat upright, and lifted one leg over the other, placing his ankle on his knee to form a figure four.

I wondered: Does the therapist have a therapist? Does that therapist have one, too?

He dressed in a light gray suit with a black V-neck, deeper than seemed appropriate, allowing his chest hairs to protrude. And he had shiny, black hair, parted on the right side, above a high-boned face with a slightly crooked nose, and so slight was his crook that, when he smiled, it caused the skin across the bridge of his nose to tighten: a tiny blemish that produced the illusion of perfection. You might look at him and think, if not for that crook, his face would be perfect, and you would be wrong, because it was precisely that crook, that tiny spot where his face was too big for its skin, which conjured the concept of perfection in the first place.

Now he leaned forward in his chair. I see, he said. We've been recommended, he said.

We?

He hummed.

It would eventually occur to me that, when speaking about my problems, the therapist would use the pronoun "we," so that he was and was not also referring to himself, maybe to humanity generally. But, in the moment, his usage of the pronoun confused me, and I wondered whether he was coercing me into playing the role of his subconscious. Or else, maybe, he was referring to me, this version of me, in the plural, a collective person—me, him, her, them, you? We didn't like it. We didn't understand it.

Now he flipped through my file, moving each loose sheet of paper from one side of the file to the other. He held his tongue in place outside of his mouth and, lifting his hand, struck his index finger against his tongue to wet it, as one strikes a match against a stone.

Okay, he said. Okay. He cleared his throat and took a sip of what I assumed was coffee from a tall thermos that rested on the coffee table between us. I will ask a few simple questions, he said. Otherwise, it's best if we just, you know, talk.

He set the thermos back on the table, then picked it up again and sipped.

I could hear people shouting outside the building—muffled voices, barely audible, barely language at all. It sounded like someone yelling unintelligibly into a pillow.

Tell me about a dream we've had recently, he said.

I hadn't dreamed in years, but I didn't want to say that. I worried about what the therapist might infer from the absence of dreams. Too much drinking. Too many sleeping pills. Failing "to process my environment." A lack of imagination.

If not dreams, he said, how about hobbies? Tell me about ourselves. What do we do outside of work?

It was getting harder and harder to call

myself a writer but, after performing my usual hesitation, I said it. I'm working on a novel.

He nodded and wrote something down and leaned forward and slurped the residual liquid from the lid of his thermos. Now he asked me what felt like a routine list of questions: What do we eat for breakfast? How are we sleeping? How much time are we spending on the internet? What do we think about before we fall asleep? How much water do we drink? The therapist was younger than me, so I struggled to tell him the truth.

It feels good, he said, to know that we are at once normal and uniquely strange.

The light was the shape of the window on the wall.

Have we been taking our medication? he said.

How did he know about the medication?

How do you know about the medication? I said.

Our file, he said.

Our file?

Here, he said. I have our file.

Oh.

Are we taking our medication? he said again.

I couldn't tell him no. I couldn't tell him that I was afraid of the side effects listed online: a loss of all motor functions, vague body aches, the inability to speak, brain fog, decreased libido, heartburn, suicidal thoughts, homicidal thoughts. I couldn't tell him that the pills made my penis

numb—like I had no penis. And the lack of a penis mocked me so that I felt the absence of my penis as a kind of presence, a phantom penis where
my real penis was. I couldn't say any of that. So, I
said sometimes.

Sometimes?

Sometimes I take them. Sometimes I forget.

We can set a reminder in our phone. We
don't have to bear that responsibility alone. The
responsibility of remembering, I mean. We have
technological assistance for remembering.

Right.

The therapist wrote in his notebook. Okay,
we are a writer, he said. How's the novel going?

I have an idea, I said. A story in mind. I just
haven't been able to get going.

I used to be an artist, he said. I wanted to be
one. An actor.

An actor?

And then—he looked down and gestured
toward himself—I became a therapist.

He closed his mouth and opened it and
closed it again, and after a long pause, realized
he wasn't going to get anything else from me, he
said, How would we describe our novel? What's
it about?

I thought about that for a while and then I
made up another story, something like this:

The novel takes place in the present day. It's
about a man, Simon, who works for a telephone
apparatus manufacturing company in Kansas.
The guy is a standard midwestern bachelor type
of guy—quiet, burly, motivated by simplicity. He

reads his Bible. He drinks. American beers, mostly local—not by choice, but because it's what one does where he lives. For the most part, he doesn't do things because he wants to do them. He lives a difficult life, full of underpaid and tedious labor, marked by occasional bouts of depression—or maybe ordinary loneliness? He can't tell the difference. He never marries. He's given up on love. He has a few friends with whom he drinks after work. He continually worries about the state of his employment. He has no transferable work skills and worries he doesn't drink enough water. He worries that hot drinks will give him stomach cancer, so each morning, when his coffee is made, he places one ice cube in his cup and waits until it fully melts before he begins to drink. He worries that he's not shitting enough. He wonders how his life might be different if he'd moved away when he had the chance. But Simon has a secret project and a productive inner life. Roughly one hundred pages into my novel, the reader discovers that Simon is also writing a novel. He's been writing it for years in his head. It's one of the weirdest books you've ever read. You have to trust me on this, I know. There's no other way to say it. He's a visionary. The novel, he's sure, is going to make him famous. For one thing, it's brilliant, intricate, and culturally relevant. The plot is massive, a maze without a center—a fantastical project, worlds within worlds. His problem, the reason why he cannot write down his ideas, however, is utterly banal. He cannot get past the first sentence. He writes it again and again. Can't get it right. It goes like this:

> *After three weeks of darkness, he — Vernon Rod-*
> *gers, whose email address was and had been the*
> *one his father gave him, vernon.vernonrodgers.*
> *rodgers@techworld.com — began to write the*
> *story of his life and death, which is to say he be-*
> *gan to write, unbeknownst to himself, his own*
> *suicide note.*

The sentence is ridiculous, right? First of all, why "three weeks"? Well, three is a holy number and must be kept. Also, the number three will have significance later in the novel when the numbers seven and thirteen, holy numbers, all come into play. He must keep three. But weeks? No, not weeks, it might be three days or three hours even. Or if it's drama he wants, then why not three years? Why not give the reader a more hyperbolic encounter and say three decades? Or lifetimes? No, not lifetimes, that's too much. It's melodramatic to say lifetimes. Three weeks is excellent, he thinks, although years does have the effect of being both symbolic and believable. Both a dream and a verisimilitude. That's what the modern-day reader wants: Believable magic. Something crazy but not too crazy. Something real but not too real. Then he asks: why "darkness"? It's a little cumbersome don't you think? Does it mean depression? Does it mean a literal nighttime? Is the dark metaphysical or scientific? The question is whether the ambiguous nature of the darkness is productive or not. Whether it contributes to the arc of the narration. Whether it is deliberate. He doesn't know what it means, but it might come to mean something later, and so he decides to keep it. Now we come to the matter of his name. It's a fine name. It's the name of a standup gentleman. A firefighter maybe. In any case, it's not the name that matters so much as the email. What is that email? Well, first, his father—also a firefighter— gave it to him when he was a child. The email introduces into the novel four things: 1) humor, 2) a pattern of repetition, 3) complacency on the part of the protagonist, and 4) the likelihood of some lingering technological incompetence. All are important to the novel, and thus the email address, no matter how stupid it sounds, must remain. Next up: "began to write." Why did he begin? Why now? And then: "the story of his life." No. Why not: the story of his death? "The story of his death" is a phrase which introduces an essential paradox into the story. How is it that he can write the story of his death? He cannot, and yet, he wants to try. He cuts the life part out. Next: "unbeknownst." It's an archaic word. Almost biblical, no? Why not simply: without knowing it. No. Clunky. It must remain unbeknownst. And anyway, this word, he hopes, will establish a playful, literary tone that the reader will come to recognize as distinctly his own, the author's. Next: "suicide note" seems redundant, right? Cut it. No, don't cut it. It's funny. Is it funny, or offensive? Keep it, for if nothing else it serves as a trigger warning, which, he thinks, is the clumsy modern-day version of foreshadowing. In addition to all this tedious editorial work, there is the problem of spellcheck and grammar check. Whenever Simon enters the sentence into Grammarly, for example, the program tells him that it contains "two critical issues" and "two advanced issues." The computer recommends cutting multiple words, words which he himself has come to love. "Own," for example, and "story." The program also recommends cutting the sentence into two or three sentences, but he fears that doing this will eliminate the "flow," as they call it, and maybe the "voice," too. Or is it the tone? He finds himself at odds with the machine that assists him in his writing. Where does his voice end and the voice of the computer begin? He critiques, again and again, every single part of the sentence, determined not to conflate his love of writing with the quality of his writing itself, and not to give in to the simplicity of his enjoyment of the written word. He shares his novel idea with one friend—Franz. Franz laughs at his struggles. It's one goddamn sentence; no one is going to care whether it's any good. Franz tries to tell him to forget the sentence and move on, but each time he tries to do this, that initial sentence, with its paradoxes and tonal slippages, haunts him. He sets out to diagram, map, and outline his novel. To trace out a grand design and to return to writing later. His house fills with sketches, drawings, charts, timelines. Graphs and notebooks. He wants to get everything in. He inscribes notes to himself all around his house and becomes consumed with the project, which deals with all

kinds of touchy contemporary topics: the politici-
zation of trauma, the rise of therapeutic nihilism,
and much more. It's going to be a tomb, he thinks.
At the level of *Gravity's Rainbow* and *Infinite Jest*
and *The Secret History*. A book with no beginning
and no end. A labyrinthine masterpiece that even
the most careful cannot navigate, a philosophical
puzzle with trap doors and dead ends. He draws
a map across the walls of his house. Maps within
maps. Plots within plots. Characters become other characters. They shed their skin, they become
each other. Vernon Rodgers is his own father. Vernon Rodgers kills himself in the past and lives to
write about it in the future, and vice versa. One
day, he's walking along the empty streets of his
small town—his head lost in the imaginary world
of his novel—when he crosses the road and is
hit and killed by an oncoming truck. Or maybe
he steps in front of the truck on purpose. It's not
clear in the writing whether his death is acciden-
tal or deliberate. I don't even know. Maybe he
doesn't know either. And that's it—the end. The
novel concludes, I think, with a final description
of his home. It's full of loose sheets of paper. In-
comprehensible designs. Unreadable charts. Poems. Secret languages. When the police enter his
house, they find nothing of interest, only the notes
of a madman. It turns out, in the end, there is no
mystery. No novel, even. Nothing but that single
stupid sentence.

The therapist wrote something down. *Interesting*, he said. He looked me up and down.

Something animal. Down, up.

It reminded me of Zeke—how Zeke had looked.

11

Two days later, I heard the gunfire again. I thought I did. I'm sure. It was the middle of the night. I heard something. Three shots. Same as before. Someone knocking at my window. Each louder than the one before. Each clearer.

I woke to the sun and the image of the sun on the floor appeared and disappeared as clouds cut across the sky. Invisible birds squawked in an invisible tree. I sat up and googled *what happened, what's happening, what happened in Berkeley, shooting in Berkeley, shooting, gunshots, Berkeley, what's happening to me right now.*

I stood by the window and watched the light accelerate and decelerate, and searched for someone to see, a person, a physical passerby—anyone who was not me to ground me there, to prove myself there. I wanted to be with someone and get out of my own head. I wanted to tell someone about what happened. To ask them about it. I thought about Janice. She would listen, wouldn't she? I counted the number of days that had passed since I didn't sleep with her. One, two. Two was enough. I texted her and she texted back immediately:

Me: want to get dinner or something?

Janice: okay, yeah

Janice: i would totally do something but not tonight i have a date

Me: np

Janice: with myself
Me: is that a thing?
Janice: is what a thing?
Janice: self-dating?
Janice: yes
Janice: obviously it's a thing
Janice: i'm going to take myself out
Janice: i'm dating myself
Janice: i'm trying to be good to myself
Janice: i write little notes and remind myself how much i love myself and ask intimate questions like what are your greatest fears and what was it like growing up in middle America, what it's like being Iranian-American in today's social climate
Janice: i light candles and make myself my favorite salad with goat cheese and cherry tomatoes sometimes
Janice: i take myself out for a movie or to a museum
Janice: it's a healing technique i'm getting to know myself better
Janice: i think i'm learning how to love myself

•

Next day, Janice invited me to meet her at SF-MOMA and check out a new exhibit on abject art. An art gallery, I was disappointed. She wanted to meet there, I figured, because conversation is not necessary at a place like that. Looking at art is easier than looking at people.

My disappointment turned into confusion when Janice arrived with Julio.

I saw her. I waved.

She looked at her shoes, at me, at her shoes. You remember Julio, she said.

Julio, yeah. Hey.

Julio offered me his hand like a dead fish, and I shook it and wiped my palm on the back pocket of my pants.

As the dynamics of our situation became clearer—two guys, one girl—my actual vision blurred. The world appeared to me as a poorly taken photograph. Had I misunderstood our arrangement? Had Janice mentioned Julio and I'd forgotten?

We bought tickets. We walked. Periodically I looked down at my broken wristwatch to make sure it was still there.

I excused myself and staggered toward the bathroom and stood before the mirror and tried to take the anxiety medication I hadn't been taking—set two pills between my teeth and ran the faucet and put my head under the running water and sucked from the stream. I gulped. But my throat tightened and closed, and the pills did not go down. I gagged and drank again and gulped, and again the pills did not go. I tasted my tongue, bitter and chalky, and I spit the pills into the trashcan and rinsed my mouth out.

Three deep breaths through my nose for a little motivation, and I walked out.

I tried not to speculate about the nature of Janice's relationship to Julio but wasn't in control of my thoughts. Julio must be her lover, potential lover, ex-lover. All possible scenarios ran through my head: boyfriend, cousin, best friend, gay friend, coworker, business partner, brother, half-brother, housemate.

Why didn't she identify their relationship right away?

Julio was much better looking than me, I could see now—a thin, lyrical type of guy, with a long neck and a misshapen Adam's apple that made him look like he had swallowed a dented ping pong ball. He had a bleach-blonde, swept-back hairstyle—an undercut with lots of length on top. His mouth was cartoonishly oversized like the Big-Mouth Snapchat filter, and he wore small shorts and a purple tank top. Often, he said the word *coalition*.

The three of us meandered silently, almost reverently, through the exhibit of abject art. There was a row of installations: smashed up teeth, flesh, orifices, trash, fast food leftovers, bloody animal fur, queasy party favors, chintzy bric-a-brac, perverse souvenirs, human hair, and abstracted testicles. A film: a woman obsessively brushes her hair until her scalp bleeds. And another: a child squirts ketchup all over her cheeks, lips, and hands. And another: a hairy man crawls into and out of a gigantic rubber hole. There were latex body parts impaled on pitchforks hanging from the ceiling. There were Barbie dolls nested in dark, kinky hair.

Against the glowing white walls, polished wood floors, high ceilings, and bright lights of the institution, the abject exhibit produced an aesthetic simultaneously sacred and profane, refined and ribald. It was like a slaughterhouse that had been recently sterilized. It reminded me of Berkeley.

Janice moved carefully, engrossed in the exhibit, mesmerized even.

I walked quickly toward the permanent collection. Julio followed me, and we moved up, circling the museum through a series of staircases and side doors and diversions.

Now Julio and I stood side by side, looking straight ahead at Robert Rauschenberg's "Erased de Kooning."

I didn't tell you, said Julio. I'm a writer, too.

No one likes writers, I joked.

I belong to a coalition of writers in Oakland. I have a novel in the works.

Yeah, I said. Everyone's writing a novel. What is it, science fiction?

No, he said. Realism.

He stuck out his neck and pointed with his head at the erased drawing. I used to admire this piece, he said. This painting. I wanted to believe that Rauschenberg was a revolutionary, that he had erased this drawing as an act of rebellion, as a rejection of the master, a protest against Abstract Expressionism and its dogmatism. But no. None of that is true. I was reading on Wikipedia that Rauschenberg had, basically, very politely, asked de Kooning for a drawing so that he could erase it. Rauschenberg even gifted de Kooning a cheap bottle of booze. He basically bought the painting, and de Kooning sold it to him, and gave him permission to do whatever he wanted. To erase the thing, and Rauschenberg did erase it, and he considered the erasure to be a poetic tribute.

I hummed.

Rauschenberg knew he wasn't as talented as de Kooning, so he reenacted the initial shock value of de Kooning's paintings, but without the object of shock. So, there's no actual art here.

I thought about that. I thought about the gunshots. But that's the whole point, I said. The absence of art is the new art.

Julio looked at me.

The most real thing is the thing that's missing, I said, though I had no idea what I was saying.

Julio moved and I followed, and we stood now in front of "The Automobile Tire Print"—one hundred feet of printer paper glued together, over which John Cage had driven his Model A after soaking its front tire in black paint.

Julio folded his arms. He said, I like this one much more. It looks like an ancient scroll.

I took out my phone and googled *interpretation of the automobile tire print*. While pretending to text someone, multitasking, speaking causally to Julio, I read aloud the results of my google search. I went, *People generally interpret the drawing as a process piece, a performance enshrined in a single, unified gesture not unlike the monoprints of more primitive art forms. Its indexical marks are representative of the structures of music and silence.*

He laughed. Did you just read that on the internet?

I laughed, too, but in a knowing way, as if I'd known that he'd known that I'd been reading from the internet. It's stupid, huh? I said, and then, eager to change the subject, I asked him about his novel.

He answered quickly as if he'd been anticipating the question. Long story short, he said. A group of scientists invents a way to 3D print DNA to correct damaged strands of DNA which have caused genetic mutations and diseases. The technology gets developed, normalized, and made readily available on the market.

Sounds like sci-fi, I said.

Eventually, he said, terrorists acquire the technology and learn how to print viruses, which they release into the populations of their enemies. Soon anyone can print viruses, especially ones for which there is no cure. All you have to do is copy the code on the internet, and the printer does the rest. This becomes a popular method of warfare, and eventually, ordinary murder. It's nearly impossible for the government to police it. It's a perfect crime. That's the backdrop of the story.

Lots of science-fantasy type stuff in there.

But it's really happening, he said.

What is?

Printing viruses. In real life.

Terrorists are printing viruses.

You don't know about that?

Well, just because something happens in a novel that also happens in real life doesn't make it realism, not really.

What makes something realism?

The absence of the capital R real, I said. (I had no clue what that meant, but was trying to conjure Josh, the shepherd.) The Real, I said, is too real to be known. We don't represent reality in art, we cover it up. We hide it. Art is a masking technique that obscures our most painful realities. Art contributes to the simplification of an all-too complex reality.

Julio was quiet.

I looked around for Janice and found her lagging, lingering to look at every piece, leaning in to see. Tightly she kept her arms folded.

Reality, I said, turning back to Julio, is the thing we cover up with art, entertainment, and news media. Real life, daily life, ordinary existence—that is the absence of reality.

You really believe that?

You don't?

He shrugged. So, what should I call my novel then?

Science fiction.

•

The phone vibrated. *Strawberries and Spinach lead the list of contaminated fruits and vegetables—click to see which other veggies may be harmful to your immediate health. A servant to the poor, or a wolf in sheep's clothing? Click to see who.*

I watched Janice approaching, painting by painting. She wore black shorts and a green, oversized military jacket, which fell below the lowest level of her shorts so that, from certain angles, she appeared not to be wearing any pants. Her hair fell just above her waistline. She examined the Erased de Kooning for several minutes, and—leaning backward and forward, looking for what was missing in the artwork—she appeared, beneath her coat, naked and not naked intermittently. Her body swayed, hypnotized. When she finally turned away, I saw that she was crying.

For the rest of the afternoon, we moved like this through the gallery: a shifting triangle, occasionally colliding together to say a few words, and then moving on to the next painting, studying—or assuming the position of studying—individual details. A boat. A cluster of dark trees. A skull.

The artwork radiated a frequency I could not tune myself to hear. One painting blended into the next, each referring to another painting I'd seen elsewhere before. The motifs, narratives, objects, faces.

Janice took pictures of the paintings and Julio took pictures of Janice taking pictures.

I felt distracted and jittery. I had no legs.

Janice leaned close to look at a painting and made a moaning sound. She seemed increasingly engrossed in each work, and this caused me to feel either ashamed of my disengagement or annoyed at Janice for her total attention to the art despite the awkwardness of our situation.

Soon Julio received a phone call and he stepped away and he lowered his head and covered his mouth to take it. Something something something. Now he hung up the phone and turned and told us he needed to leave. He needed to prepare dinner for the members of his co-op and it was his turn to cook this week and he needed to buy the tofu bean burgers.

Janice and Julio hugged goodbye, and he whispered something in her ear and she smiled.

I lifted a hand to say goodbye to him, though he didn't reciprocate.

•

Now that Julio was gone, I stayed close to Janice. I put on a look: casual, casually contemplating the paintings in front of me, nothing too serious. I squinted and nodded as if in approval of something no one said. And I could see in my peripheral vision: Janice squinted to look at a different painting, the one next to the one I squinted at.

After a long pause, I said: How do you know him?

Julio? He's a partner, she said, and walked away.

Oh. I noted the ambiguous "a" article. I pointed to an empty canvas—totally blank, no paint at all.

What do you think of this one? I said.

The affect is hard to describe, she said. It's almost sexual but precedes sexuality. It's lighter. Almost innocent. Youthful, you might say, but with a tinge of despair, or dread. It's the moment before experience ossifies into the imagery of experience.

Was she making fun of me?

•

After an hour or so, we left the gallery and walked in the city. The weather was fine. Lukewarm. The streets crowded and noisy. I saw a man pissing in a park and another man watching him piss.

Enough time had passed since I brought up Julio that I felt I could bring him up again. There was a lull in our conversation, and I asked, neglecting to insert a subject into the sentence: So, like a business partner?

Janice looked at me.

Your partner.

She laughed, kind of.

Julio, I mean.

I'm polyamorous, remember?

Polygamist?

Polyamorous. I'm in several relationships, she said. Some sexual, some not. I mentioned it at the party. Remember?

I didn't remember.

I mentioned it, she said. Didn't I mention it?

No, she hadn't.

Remember?

Right, I said. Of course. I remember. You're polyamorous. That's awesome.

She looked at me.

What?

Why are you making that face?

I'm not, I said. There's no face. No face. See? (I made a face.)

Don't be weird about it, she said.

My brain produced a fog that caused me to

remain silent for what felt like several minutes, unable to access my thoughts.

There are lots of different reasons why people do it, she said. For me, I don't know—. I don't believe in love, not like that. I believe in love in general, if love means altruism, goodness, and compassion, but not the kind of love that we get from nationalism and Netflix. It's romantic love I don't believe in. I read somewhere that it was invented by poets and marketers and religions people to domesticate or tame sexual desire.

I nodded and kicked a small rock into the street.

I could tell Janice wanted to talk about this. I let her talk.

She went on about the ethics of polyamorous love, speaking more quickly than I had heard her speak before. It was a quickness which gave her language a rehearsed quality. Her voice got louder and clearer and suddenly firm.

And for the record, she was saying now, I practice egalitarian, ethical, solo polyamory. I'm almost more of a polysexual, you know, I'll fuck anything human, but that's not quite right either. There's no category for it.

No categories, of course.

Janice went on. She took out her phone and looked at it, and scrolled up and down the screen, and continued to talk.

I zoned out and took out my phone, too, and searched for Janice's dating profile online. When I found it, it revealed what I should have already known: *Tech writer. Tech mystic. Sex adventurer.*

Marketing manager and creative content creator. My selves are Poly, SSC, GGG, NSA, ISO-whatever, and WAA. I have many, ever-changing wants, needs and feelings. I'm open to all kinds of relationships — friends, friends with benefits, fuckbuddies, part-time boyfriends/girlfriends/partners, long-time on-and-off lovers. I believe sex is a basic human need, like food and sleep, and nothing more.

This is the last time I will see her, I thought. And I promised myself, in that moment, that I wouldn't call her again—not because I objected to polyamory, but because I felt exhausted just thinking about it. It seemed complicated and emotionally demanding. Or maybe not. Maybe I did have a problem with polyamory because it seemed too easy, one of many acceptable, countercultural, California lifestyles. Or maybe I subconsciously envied polyamory, and I imagined it to offer a hidden pleasure from which I was excluded. Maybe I even harbored a deep-seated hatred for polyamory. Whatever my reasoning, I decided, then, that Janice wasn't worth pursuing if I had to navigate the dynamics of a multi-partner relationship. I had no experience with non-monogamy and felt too old to try. But even this decision, in the moment I made it, felt routine, predetermined, as if made by a former version of myself. Who am I in the future, and will I be the kind of person who would venture into polyamorous love? Why wouldn't I want to see her again, if only for conversation and casual sex? I had no one else to see. No other prospects. I wondered— as Janice enthusiastically enumerated the virtues of a multi-person love—whether I unwittingly lay the groundwork for some inevitable irony, as in: he says he won't, but we know he will. As in: he wants what he wants whether he likes it or not.

I tuned back into the conversation. Janice was explaining something. I have more than one partner at a time, she said, but don't consider myself to be part of any couples. I don't have primary partners. It's an independent life.

Of course.

Anyway, she said, what I meant to say is that I didn't want Julio to come to the gallery today. He invited himself.

I nodded.

He wanted to hang out with you because he's trying to get over this jealousy thing he has. Getting to know your partner's partners is supposed to help with that. Not that you and I are partners. I'm just saying—.

•

We went home separately, or I went home, and Janice stayed in the city. She had other plans, she had said, to see someone else. I didn't ask who. None of it mattered. I'll never see her again, I thought. She isn't even real.

And still, that night, thoughts of Janice kept me awake—something about her. Something. Fantasies of her filled my head. Not sexual fantasies, but domestic ones. Visions of the prosaic and the mundane—of making dinner and watching HBO and brushing our teeth together before bed. Dreams of living together somewhere else in time and space, a suburban life, a garden, a lawn-mower, a garage.

You're sick.

Sometime between two and three in the morning, I heard someone in the hallway. Someone moving, heavy and loud, just outside my door. Coming closer.

I sat up.

Think of something else.

The hallway light lit up the space beneath my door, enough light to give the objects in my room an outline, a vague shape.

I waited until the movement stopped and all was quiet again. I didn't want to get out of bed, but now I needed to pee and knew I wouldn't be able to fall asleep until I did. My body dragged itself and my heels stiffened, and it took me a few seconds to balance myself before moving. I put my hand on the foot of the bed and stumbled out.

When I got to the bathroom, the door was shut. I knocked. No answer. I knocked again. I walked inside. The light was on, and now I could see. There. The floor was covered in blood—blood on the toilet seat, smeared on the bath rug and around the shower, not yet dried, permeating toward my bare feet, as if its source was beneath the floor, or was the floor itself. It was much more blood than would come from a nosebleed or a small cut or an extracted tooth. The blood was dark, the color of dirt.

I thought to cry out for help but feared I would be blamed for the bleeding.

Bleeding? No. It's not blood, it's shit. Fleshy excrement. Or no. Not shit. Vomit. It must be vomit. Someone—a housemate, a friend of a housemate—must have come into the bathroom and tried to throw up but missed the toilet entirely and heaved onto the floor, probably more than once, someone too drunk to realize they had missed the toilet, too drunk to clean up, someone with an enormous stomach, vomited across the floor.

I pretended I hadn't seen anything and walked back to my room and removed a plastic water bottle from my recycling bin and peed into it. I drank whiskey from the bottle and got back into bed.

The phone vibrated. *A neurologist explains why we see a story about the world—a story—and not the real deal. How a single mother was tortured to death in her own backyard. How one family built an underground sex trafficking operation out of their basement in Salt Lake City, Utah.*

PART TWO

12

Of course I saw Janice again. Why wouldn't I? She was exciting and interesting and unpredictable. The question was, why did she want to see me again?

Two days after meeting her in San Francisco, we met at an overpriced Mexican restaurant near my place.

I watched her watching her reflection in the windows as we walked inside.

We sat in a diner-style booth in the back and looked down at our menus. Janice ordered two beers and a plate of vegan nachos.

The waiter said, Thanks, treasure, and took the menus.

I told Janice that I was a vegan too and she seemed happy about that, but not as happy as I had hoped she'd be.

The restaurant was poorly lit and crowded with graduate students and professors, and people who looked like graduate students and professors but surely weren't. The music was up, and we had to speak at a volume slightly louder than comfortable. We discussed the spectrum of topics: TV shows, podcasts, dieting, dating, new beers we had been wanting to try, how our friends were getting divorced and rescuing dogs and having kids or not having kids. Janice spoke easily and without pause as if she had rehearsed everything she had to say. She stirred her drink with her fingers and leaned in. She asked me for the facts. All the facts.

The facts?

Yes, she wanted the facts. Now that we had made it past the initial stages of getting to know each other, it was time for the facts. All the facts. The word sounded like *fucks* when she said it. *Give me all the fucks.*

The facts: I grew up in the middle of nowhere in the Midwest, in the plains, in the snow. That's why my face looks like this, I said. I'm not as old as my face is. But back then I was always squinting. I had to squint to see.

Janice reached across the table and traced the lines on my forehead and around my mouth. I like it, she said. Your face. You look extreme. Severe. Like Sean Penn.

I had the impulse to tell her that I thought the same thing about her face, that it was old, older than her body suggested it should be. But I didn't.

More facts: Jewish mother. Catholic father. First, I was the Catholic kid at a Jewish school. Later, I was the Jewish kid at the Catholic school. I was doomed to believe and not to believe in God. My father died a long time ago and my mother remarried and moved to Maine.

More facts: I went to graduate school to become a writer.

Are you writing now?

I'm trying. (I didn't tell her that I hadn't been writing in years. I didn't tell her that I tended to get disoriented and confused by my own writing.

I would sit down to write and become fidgety. I would question myself, my feelings and the feelings behind my feelings, and the construction of my sentences, and the meaning of individual words. Sometimes, I would lose the narrative and forget where I was and what I had been doing, and in the absence of any kind of creative output I would think about other things: the cynicism of culture, the fragility of the human body, the tedium of social life and work, or the accumulation of wealth and the attendant clout I imagined it would bring me.) But I moved to Berkeley six months ago because I needed to get out and Parker got me a gig at a startup, bottom of the payroll, and I work from home.

Tell me something that's wrong with you.

Wrong with me?

Something is wrong with everyone. What's wrong with *you*?

I don't know.

Don't be shy.

Okay. I'm epileptic.

You have seizures?

I nodded.

Janice ordered a second round of beer.

I asked her the same questions she asked me, and she gave me the answers. She talked about her family, her childhood. She was born in Chicago, went to University of Chicago, studied marketing, and got a gig in advertising out of college. She told me about how her father was in the Army, and her mother an Iranian immigrant. I have a fractured identity, she said. Two opposing energies compete for my heart. She told me that her mother had abandoned them at a young age, when she first arrived in the United States. So that was us, she said: mom, dad and me. Three, and later two, and then one. The family fracturing was a source of guilt and confusion, because—as she put it—she was an Iranian woman raised by a single white man. And not just any white man, she said. He was all military. Very military.

Very, oh.

Hardcore, she said. Intense. Self-sacrificing, but in a condescending, martyr-type of way. Macho. I never saw him cry. And he ate the same thing for breakfast every morning. Grape nuts. Grape nuts and coffee. Black coffee. And he drank black beer and he never talked about what he liked and didn't like. Everything was neutral to him. Everything was given, and his reaction to everything was blank.

He sounds like a jerk, I said unthinkingly, pandering to what I assumed were Janice's daddy issues.

No, she said. He was quiet, that's all. But he was gentle and soft spoken. Don't misunderstand. He was sad. Everyone's sad, I know, but he was broken. He didn't say much because he didn't want to say the wrong thing. He didn't want to talk about what he didn't understand, and he didn't understand much. That's what he told me. Better to shut your mouth, that's what he said. He used to say: what's gone is gone forever, and that's the hardest thing to learn. He didn't trust his feelings, or any feelings for that matter. I don't think he really knew who he was or what he believed in. And once I finished college and settled with a job and an apartment, he shot himself in the head. Right in the mouth.

Jesus Christ.

But I consider it to be a generosity toward me because, I think, he waited to do it until I was gone—he waited to do what he had wanted to do for his entire adult life.

I'm sorry, I said, reached out to touch her hand, set it flat on the table in front of her, but she pulled it away and placed it in her lap, and I, in turn, pretended to swat away a fly.

The lunch hour ended, and the restaurant started to clear out and the chatter quieted, and the clank of plates and silverware grew louder. Janice crossed one leg over the other, and then reversed her legs, and placed the other leg over the one, and undid them and put both feet flat on the floor, and leaned backward, and then leaned forward and put her elbows on the table. She drank.

She licked her lips and put her pointer finger on the napkin in front of her and spun it in tight circles on the table. She kept talking. I let her talk. She told me about how she moved to California after her dad died to get access to the sun and the open space. She got an apartment in Oakland and a marketing job in the city, then bounced around Silicon Valley. I earnestly believed, she said, that moving to the west coast would heal me. The sea and the sun. But when my dad was gone, I couldn't sit still or settle down. I rejected sleep, too. I was afraid, she said, that I wouldn't be able to wake up again. That I'd not be able to come back. I feared not being there in the morning. Even now, she added, I don't like sleeping. I have to force myself into it.

I know that feeling.

I take sleeping pills and drink or turn on the television or the white noise machine or the fan, just for the proof of something there. Anything. A meaningless drone. I read cheap paperbacks, crap detective novels or erotica until I fall asleep, mid-sentence, with all the lights on. And even now I usually wake up with a sense of relief, thankful to have made it out alive.

13

Weeks went by. I spent more and more time with Janice. We still hadn't had sex or even kissed. We talked and didn't talk and looked at each other. We went to dinner. We danced in bars. We made popcorn and watched movies. Movies goddamnit, not films. Janice hated films. Films are what white people watch, she said. Fuck films. She referred to everything, therefore—even YouTube clips or Instagram stories—as movies.

Occasionally, I walked her to work, and we had coffee together. Janice was generous and non-judgmental, so much so that I often took her all-accepting attitude for indifference and flippancy, which caused me to act alternately tense and relaxed with her. I told myself that because Janice was seeing other people, I should feel no pressure to be everything usually required of a romantic partner—sexy, smart, charming, witty, and all that. But telling myself to feel no pressure created a new pressure to feel no pressure. And so it went.

Janice told me her secrets. It was easy for her. There seemed to be, for her, no difference between thinking and speaking. She held nothing back and didn't consider anything to be private or sacred. She was unashamed. She made fun of herself. She opened her mouth and laughed and threw her head back and showed her long neck. I peed my pants on an airplane while taking a nap, she said. I search for myself every morning on the internet. I cry during Google commercials. At night, I jump onto my bed because I'm still afraid of what's underneath it. I cry for no reason. I act like I'm stretching so I can smell my armpits. I pretend to text on my phone while secretly taking a zillion selfies.

She told me crude stories about gym showers, library hallways, and public bathrooms. She told me that she used to be a kleptomaniac, that she stole things from people, random things, things useless to her, meaningless objects and such—a child's tricycle, a plumber's screwdriver, a soccer coach's cleats.

Why?

What mattered to me, she said, is that I could take something, anything. And by taking something I felt like I had some control over my life. I still need that feeling.

•

Once a week we left the East Bay and drove away into the city or farther north or south. Sometimes we took the day and drove to the coast and stood at the water where the earth seemed to extend forever. We went east, too. Into the hills. It felt good to go, to be gone, to escape routine.

It's better, Janice said, to run away from your problems rather than solving them. Problem solving is an institutional imperative. Better to escape. Better to escape in the middle of the night and get out before anyone notices.

There was a restaurant we liked east of

Berkeley, up on a ridge somewhere. It was quiet there, and it had a view. We recognized no one, and no one recognized us.

What do you do for work? I asked. You can tell me now.

She grinned and covered her mouth. I'm a writer, too.

Uh, oh.

I'm in tech. I write dialogue.

Dialogue?

For robots.

Robots.

Sex robots.

Oh.

For the pornographic revolution.

I asked her to explain.

So, yeah, the robots have sex with each other, she said. She made air quotes around the word sex.

What does the human do?

Nothing, she said. No humans.

I didn't understand.

The human is nothing, she said. The human is irrelevant. Soon, every consumer will have a customized sex robot. One robot per person. Like a smartphone. Everyone will have a smartphone and a sex robot. It's not a full body sex robot. It's just the lower half, the groin, the crotch area, complete with life-size sex parts.

How do they speak to each other?

Speak?

You said you write dialogue, but how do they talk to each other if they don't have mouths?

She laughed. You don't need a mouth to say something, she said. This is how it works. You take two robots, yours and someone else's, put them together, turn them on and that's it.

That's it?

That's it, she said. Because sex or the possibility of sex has the potential to ruin the relationship that allows sex to be possible in the first place.

I made a face.

The robots have sex with each other so that we don't have to, she said. They attend to the psychological realities of sex and relieve us from the burdens of needing sex. They act as a surrogate for you and your sex life. They have sex for you when you can't have it. No one ever never needs to have sex again.

Wait—.

Let's think of a few scenarios, Janice said. For the robots.

Okay.

Okay. Scenario One. Take our current situation. You and me. We met each other under the pretense of a possible hookup. It's likely that when we planned our get-together, we considered, maybe even fantasized about hooking up. Let's admit that. Soon this gets confusing. For example, when I told you I wanted to meet for lunch, maybe you thought lunchtime meetings mean no sex. But admit it, part of you hoped that maybe we'd have a quickie at my apartment, or that I'd give you a hand job in the park. The sexual tension causes you to focus on yourself, even now, as we speak.

Maybe you're asking yourself, How does my hair look? Am I saying the right thing? Should I have made that joke? Why won't she make eye contact with me? Does it mean anything that she ordered nachos for lunch? Not an ideal pre-sex food. Blah, blah. In short, the possibility of sex inhibits sex. We're on edge. We need to loosen up a bit, you know. Okay. Now imagine that we have our sex robots. Let's say that the first thing we do when we meet each other—the very first thing—is put our sex robots together. We watch them grind it out, at first slowly, and then fast and explosive. Eventually, both climax. And that's it. From that point on, both of us are free. We have vicariously orgasmed without the anxieties and emotional attachment associated with new sex partners. The pressure of sex is gone. We can discuss politics and religion without worrying about whether we're going to get lucky at the end of the date. We can talk openly. We can be honest.

I had the urge to spit but swallowed instead.

Scenario Two. Let's say we had been dating for a few weeks and you suddenly get very nervous. Let's say you found out something about my past that intimidates you—maybe that I used to identify as a lesbian or a man. Maybe you found out that I used to be a sex worker and that I'd fucked hundreds or thousands of men.

Thousands?

And let's say that this knowledge caused performance anxiety for you, because, I don't know, maybe you're repressed, and suddenly, despite weeks of good sex, you are incapable of getting an erection. Even the slightest reminder of my past is enough to distract you. Occasionally your cock gets hard enough, but you almost always lose it—emasculation, shame, blah, blah. Enter the sex robots. Instead of having sex, now we watch our robots have sex. Your robot is the ubermensch. It never loses its hard-on, never fails to satisfy its counterpart robot. You slowly gain your confidence, and our sex life resumes. It turns out, sex is nothing intimidating or mysterious, nothing more than a mechanism. You get it?

I'm a little slow, I think.

Okay. Scenario Three. Let's pretend that you and I got married.

Married, great.

For a few years, our marriage is good, the sex is mostly good, sometimes it's average, but that's expected. Both of us eventually get busy with our careers. You're getting a new job. I'm nearing a promotion. We don't have the time or concentration required to have good sex. We might try here and there, but each time we do, you're thinking about the progress of your work, and I'm worried about turning in my quarterly reports on time. You see where this is going. Both of us begin to feel guilty for not having sex as much as we used to. We agree we should be having more sex. We hear our coworkers talking about the sex they're having, even in older age. We begin to conflate our sex life for our most basic feelings toward each other, wondering whether we care about each other as much as we used to. What will we do?

Sex robots?

Sex robots. Each morning, let's say, we let our robots do their thing, and boom, our sex lives are restored. The psychological burden of sex is gone and we can entirely focus on our careers without wondering about the state of our marriage. We don't have to have sex if we don't want to. There's nothing antisocial about it. We have the robots, you see? A person has a limited source of libido at any given time. And libido is a powerful source of motivation and sometimes we need to focus that libido on things other than our sexual partner. The sex robots allow us to participate in the act of sex—thus fulfilling familial, social, or consumer demands of it—while also reserving our libido as a vibrant life-source that fuels our careers and creative projects. It's revolutionary. It will free up our minds to think of things other than sex. The robots satisfy the more deep-seated psychological aspects of sex, things like power, revenge, self-actualization, self-harm, social status, and the kind of violence and aggression that comes from failing to actualize what one believed should be a normative and satisfying sex life. Just think about it. If everyone had a good sex life—the kind of sexual habits that we consider not only healthy, but essential—we would have a much better political reality, too. Why do you think all of these white supremacists are marching in the streets? Because they're a bunch of nerds that never have sex, right? Why do you think so many leaders of rightwing movements discourage young men from masturbating? Because they want to channel the sexual frustrations of young men for political purposes. When we introduce these robots into the market, when they become as common as a cellphone or laptop, you'll see a significant decrease in political polarization, domestic violence, sexual harassment, rape, STDs. And we'll see fewer angry men, too. Wait for it.

14

Days later. Janice leaned down and stretched and stuck out her neck to drink her cocktail without using her hands. Her hair was up in a beehive shape thing, a pineapple look. She sucked a piece of ice and chewed it and rested her elbow on the bar and set her head in the palm of her open hand. With her free hand, she reached over and grabbed me by the wrist and pushed it down in what would have seemed, in other circumstances, to be an act of aggression. The skin of her arm was thin, and her veins protruded, blue and darker blue. She breathed deeply and held her breath and exhaled. Abruptly she said, *what are we?*

The more I got to know Janice, the more I became grateful for this tendency in her—the tendency to disambiguate things by naming them. To make verbal boundaries and contracts. As if the reality of a thing depended on the words that define it.

Are we friends? she said. Or more?

More is good, I said.

Should we sleep together?

Blood rushed to my head. Tonight?

Not tonight, she said. I have work early in the morning and I don't want to lose sleep. Plus, my roommate's parents are visiting from Pennsylvania. So, we'd have to sleep at your house, and I'd rather not.

What's wrong with my house?

Nothing, she said. But not on a weekday. I like to sleep in my own bed. I worry that I'll forget something. Toothbrush. Medication. Pajamas.

Right.

Saturday, she said.

Now I felt a sense of deflated excitement. I started picking at the scab on my calf—the wound I did and didn't inflict on myself earlier.

Okay, I said. Saturday.

15

On Saturday it was raining. The first rain since the end of summer. A bad one. A deluge that fell slantwise with the wind, pounding against the roof in rhythmic bursts. The house shook with it. It heaved and cracked and seemed to break. The windows convulsed and the walls shuddered, and the curtain rings rattled the steel rod where they hung. Somehow, I felt comforted by the storm—by the physical evidence of wreckage. The visibility of deterioration and destruction. It felt correct to witness the world as it had been on the news: dangerous and unpredictable and nearing its inevitable end.

All morning I watched YouTube videos. *Ten misconceptions about polyamory. The underbelly of refugee camps. How eleven people control the world.* The videos they kept playing, one after the other. I didn't have to click anything. I watched a video about the Denver International Airport, New Coke, Deepwater Horizon, Alternative Therapy suppression, collapsing media conglomerates, the porn industry, and the rise of Satanism in western governments. I watched a video about Antifa, yes—how it was secretly funded by conservative strategists to make the Left look like a bunch of crazies. Was it true? Probably not. Who could know. The internet is operated—isn't it?— by algorithms and bots, fake people with fake identities moving their fake cursors, clicking fake websites and liking fake pictures. The only real things were the ads and the products they advertised. The problem with the internet, Parker told me once, is that so many people are experimenting with alter-egos. Adults become children again and, what's even scarier, is that children pretend to be adults.

•

When the storm passed, I walked to Janice's. The streets were cleared out—empty, and the gutters ran full of rainwater. As I went, I heard the words of the therapist: Before we do anything, visualize that thing in our mind. We must achieve our goals mentally before we can achieve them physically. It was for this reason that I began to play and replay potential sex scenarios with Janice. Most of these scenarios were conventional. Others were mildly adventurous. But soon, my mind, of its own accord, began to play out a different scene—one where I started doing things wrong. Bad things. Faux pas. Miscalculations. Assumptions. I tried to stop thinking, to stop the scenes from playing out, but they kept rolling anyway.

In one scene: Janice and I were making out, in the dark—playfully, but with intention. And I, in the fantasy or nightmare, interpreted this situation as an invitation to keep going—to go further. And my imagination went further, too. Janice touched my leg, my inner thigh. And I saw in this a sign of readiness and progression. And we

114

began, and she seemed into it, moaning and such, and occasionally saying some raunchy thing—a line from her sex robots, maybe. And then I did something wrong. I stuck my finger in her mouth and made a fishhook, put my hands around her neck, pulled her hair, put my finger in her asshole. Suddenly, Janice promptly ended the encounter and told me to leave—get out, she said. And later, after I'd left, she called me out on Twitter, posted messages on social media, warning other women about me. She wrote that I was insensitive and forceful.

A trial ensued.

The presiding judge looked down at me. What the hell did you think you were doing? Do you think that you had permission to choke her like that, to use the fishhook?

I barely even used the fishhook, I said. I just put my finger in her mouth for effect, to show her that if she wanted me to do the fishhook, I could. And I was willing. It's normal, isn't it? Doesn't everyone use the fishhook?

And now, presently, walking, my imagined scenario caused me to feel real shame. My imagination had become real. I felt it. I felt awkward even then, in total isolation, cut off from the social sphere. I was all foggy in the head, and I had to sit down to gather my thoughts. What thoughts? Who put those thoughts there?

You're sick.

•

Janice's apartment building was a glass structure in central Berkeley. It had been designed in the 90's to anticipate, it seemed like, what people must have imagined buildings would look like in a then-distant future, which, in the present tense, looked like the now-distant past.

She lived on the first floor, third door on the right. I knocked five times and held my breath and dried off my hands on the back of my jeans and took out my phone and pretended to do something on it.

Janice answered in her exercise clothes. I had never seen her so stripped down. Everything about her was small. She wore tiny spandex shorts and a crop top the same color as her skin—beige, oatmeal, faun, biscuit—which made her look androgynous and humanoid and without nipples.

You're early, she said.

I apologized.

She kissed me on the mouth and invited me in. I have a few more sets, you don't mind.

I sat on the couch.

Janice positioned herself on the floor, laying herself flat and cracking back her head to look at me.

I looked at my wristwatch. I looked at my phone.

She started her burpees.

Her apartment had two bedrooms and two baths and gave off the feeling of an upscale hotel lobby. The mode was mid-century modern, arranged with sleek shapes—orange accent chairs, a glass Platner dining table, an artichoke chandelier.

A balcony looked down on the street below.

Janice was panting now, drawing short and rapid breaths. She made her little mouth into an O.

I went into the bathroom and ran the faucet and splashed cold water on my face and looked at myself in the mirror. The eyes sagged. The mouth went lopsided. I threw more water onto my face again and put my head beneath the faucet and drank and I rubbed some of Janice's face lotion on my cheeks and went out again.

Do you have coffee?

She went, mm-hm—down and up. The Nespresso pods are in the left cupboard there, above the machine.

I put the Nespresso pod in the machine, removed a small mug from the cupboard and set it in the place beneath the nozzle. I pressed the button on the espresso maker, and it released an excremental discharge, thick brown liquid dripped into the porcelain mug. I moved my eyes back and forth from the mug to the nozzle, so as not to let them wander toward Janice, who was still bouncing. I guzzled the americano while standing at the counter. It burned my tongue. Then I remembered a detail from the story I had told the therapist—about a correlation between too-hot coffee and stomach cancer—and I ran over to the sink and rinsed out my mug, and filled it with water and guzzled that, too. Then I repeated it: filled the mug and guzzled the water. And again. Three times in total. I hoped that the cold water would counteract the hot coffee in my throat and stomach.

I took out my phone to look through the news, but I couldn't focus while Janice was still breathing like that, almost panting.

Watch TV if you want, she said.

TV. Okay.

The TV wasn't a TV at all, but a large computer monitor that sat atop the coffee table and faced the couch.

How do I turn this on?

Janice got up and stood over me. I could smell her sweat—a subtle odor, a weedy little onion. She grabbed a remote and pressed something and the screen flared up. She typed something into the search engine and entered a password.

There you go.

Nothing was on television. I flipped through the channels nervously and eventually settled on a college football game I didn't care about. The University of Iowa versus Whoever.

All done, Janice said, finishing her last push-up. Going to take a shower.

I hoped she would invite me to join her, but she didn't. I turned off the TV and was alone. Somewhere outside a dog barked, and another dog barked, and another. Through the window: traffic—a procession of headlights passing through the fog in a rumble of wet tires. Thunder shook the apartment, one clap and another. Briefly I forgot where I was; I lost all sense of place, and I struggled to recompose myself, to replay the circumstances that brought me there—the shape of the room and the curvature of the couch and the angle of the refracted light coming into the glass door at a deluge, a blowout. I heard strange creaking noises, psychic projections of noises previously heard—the sound of my own body, and the pause between breaths. I thought I was going to have a seizure, so I went to my bag and took my medication and drank another glass of water.

Dizziness. Voices in the other room. Janice? I said, but Janice was not there.

The phone vibrated. *Male suicide rates at an all-time high. 49 murdered by terrorist groups. Fascists in Ukraine to ignite a race war. Russia preparing to invade. Here's your guide to the newest Netflix releases: which ones you should be watching. One dead and three injured at Synagogue shooting in California. Are you addicted to the news cycle? Here's our weekly recommended coping exercises.*

Now Janice emerged from the bathroom in a fluffy pink robe. I was about to make soup, she said. Want some?

Soup?

Curry, she said. Power curry.

Janice vanished into the walk-in pantry and came out a few seconds later clutching a bag of sweet potatoes and curry powder. She opened the refrigerator and opened one of its drawers and removed a head of broccoli and a bundle of asparagus and went back into the pantry and came out carrying a bag of garlic cloves, a bag of tomatoes, one giant red onion, and a bottle of olive oil. She removed the vegetables from the bags and set them out one by one onto the counter and took a cutting board from a cupboard above the refrigerator and two knives, one small blade and one large, from their block. She minced the garlic with the smaller blade and sliced the sweet potatoes with the larger one. She cut kale and carrots, and placed tomatoes into a large pot to boil, and went back to the refrigerator to get some parsley. She chopped it. I watched her cook, moving with ease and deliberation. She chopped and sliced and cut faster now. The knife was louder on the cutting board like a hammer falling. She tore bits of broccoli apart, ripped the stems off the asparagus and she threw things into the pot.

The water boiled and spilled over, and Janice stirred it again.

We pushed our way through ten minutes of conversation: weirdest taco trucks in Oakland, best Alejandro Jodorowsky movies.

Soon the meal was ready to eat, and Janice spooned the soup into two bowls, threw some salt and pepper on and drizzled some olive oil across. She turned off the kitchen lights, and the overhead, so that the computer screen was the only light in the room.

We ate on the couch. The curry soup was good and salty. It had been a long time since I'd eaten anything other than little microwave meals.

Janice finished her soup quickly, and asked whether I wanted anymore, and when I said maybe later, she set her bowl on the coffee table and leaned over and put her head between my chest and armpit.

Want to lie down and watch a movie?

We went into her room and I threw myself,

knees and ribcage, down on the bed.

The bedroom, like the living room, was spare, surface-level, meant for living in, and nothing more. A single set of drawers, bedside table, unpainted Ikea desk, and a womb chair in the corner. Even the bed was uninviting, too firm, too high: I sat; my feet hung above the floor.

Horror? Janice said.

What is?

Are you down to watch a horror movie?

Horror, I said. Sure.

Janice took her MacBook from the desk drawer, plugged it into a nearby cord, opened the screen and logged into her Netflix account. Dracula?

Dracula. Good.

We watched Dracula.

The movie was nothing special, and the acting was mostly average. I watched though, as well as I could, waiting for the movie to show me something about the world, the way it was or was becoming.

Dracula sucked the blood of beautiful men and women and he got younger and more beautiful himself, though he wasn't *that* beautiful, not as beautiful as Julio.

During a particularly violent scene—Dracula ravishing an entire convent somewhere in Eastern Europe—Janice leaned across and put her face on my face. We kissed, though it felt wrong to kiss then, while Dracula was eating.

My wayward fantasy—the nightmare, really, as it became—still lingered in the background of my thoughts, inhibiting my movements. I slowed and tensed up, but managed to progress, albeit awkwardly, from one sexual stage to the next: kissing to touching, touching to holding to holding down. Maybe I appeared overeager when I took my shirt off—which I did, I admit, unprompted and instinctually, not because I necessarily wanted to take it off, but it's what one does—because Janice jolted back, and that caused me to jolt, too.

Dracula was sucking.

Janice placed both her hands on my chest and squeezed—the way that a man might grip a woman's breasts and twisted my nipples until they hardened, and she stuck her tongue into my ear. Tell me, she whispered now, what you want me to do to you. And I did tell her. I was not yet past the initial awkwardness of having taken off my shirt, so I could only bring myself to say generic, boring things. Touch that, I said. Oh, yeah, yeah. I hesitated to say anything too specific— anything Janice might use as fodder for her sex robot dialogues.

We performed our duties quietly, gently, as if participating in an exchange of goods. A transaction of pleasure, like for like. When Janice had done her work, I took my turn. I turned her over, all nonthreatening, and fooled around: tongue, one finger, two now, now the hook, twelve o'clock, two and a half inches below the urethra, the come hither and all that, right around the corner. And I moved onto other things, too, and at each stage, I asked Janice, as the internet instructed me to do: Is this okay? Is that? Is this? And with each question, Janice answered businesslike: yes, yes, yes. There were so many yeses that I lost track of which ones were referred to questions and which indicated pleasure.

And Dracula was there, too—shedding his skin to become a wolf, and then to become a bat, and then a man again. His eyes went red.

How long had we been going now?

I tried to distract myself. I looked at a clock mounted on the wall. It was a replica of a Piet Mondrian painting—a grid of solid colors, whites and yellows, and a large red square panel in the center. But that clock was the opposite of a Mondrian; it ascribed to the painting the very use-value which the artist originally aimed to strip away. The clock instrumentalized what Mondrian had wanted to render nonfunctional.

I was brought back to the present when Janice started to talk loudly. She was talking dirty: *fuck, wet,* etc. But she spoke in the third person, so that her sex talk sounded like narration, rather than description or instruction. *He likes it,* she said. *He wants it rough,* she said. *He needs it. He pulls her hair.* I understood the narration—because it named both characters in the third person, and therefore, it seemed, lacked interiority—to be an omniscient third person. And if this narration was all-knowing, what else might she say? What did she know that I didn't?

He isn't as hard as he used to be, the narrator might say. *He's not as strong. Not as young and smooth and tenacious. He's losing it now. Look at him.*

And I began to experience the present moment in the third person, too. As "he"—himself. My perspective shifted to a position off the bed, away from the act of intercourse, and when I looked back, he was not me having sex with Janice, but someone else entirely and I watched the sex that I was supposed to be having.

Go faster, he thought, eager to get to the end. *He goes faster.*

Now I had a little vision, a daydream. The sex robots: a mechanical penis and a mechanical vagina, moving forward and backward toward a preprogrammed outcome. Then I saw endless mechanical penises. A whole valley of robotic cocks and balls, all of them swinging up and down in unison, into and out of their mechanized counterparts.

Don't lose it, I thought, and lost it. I slipped out. A dark and sluggish tool. Slumped against her inner thigh. A fishy smell with garlic and ammonia. Better to come early than not at all. Better to fake it than to fail. So, I did. I pretended to orgasm, and I cried out, as if for help, in a voice I could not recognize as my own. It was a shrill sound, a broken car horn.

I stood and wiped myself off with my undershirt, though there was nothing to wipe. Then I collapsed onto the bed next to Janice and exhaled. I wanted to be far away.

Janice reached over and touched me. Lay with me, she said. She kissed me in a way that was probably loving, but which seemed belittling.

For a while, we lay prone and supine, talked and didn't talk, converged and faded into thinness and silence. Our feet hung off the bed. The screen went deep blue. It felt like I was underwater.

16

I woke up to pee in the middle of the night and the room was darker than when I had fallen asleep. I rolled out of bed and went toward where I thought the bathroom was but wasn't—that was the closet. I turned around and lifted my arms and stretched them out, Frankenstein-like, and shuffled one foot in front of the other without taking either off the ground. When I found the bathroom, I made sure the door was shut behind me before I turned on the light. I recoiled from it and allowed my eyes to reopen in their own time and sat on the toilet and pissed like a girl, as I was still half-erect and needed to be pressed down.

I looked at my wristwatch and stood and examined the bathroom, hunting for clues. Clues for what? I didn't know. I opened the mirror cabinet behind the sink and found: French toothpaste, French perfume, a ring-holder dish in the shape of the Eiffel Tower, contraceptive pills, generic painkillers, and a bottle of antidepressants (different than my own antidepressants) and another medication I didn't recognize.

Taped to the back of the mirror was a drawing, sketched out, I guessed, by Janice herself. It was two faces. The first was the universal smiley face: a circle, two dot-sized eyes and a U-shape mouth (no nose) beneath which was written in bold: medication. The second face was drawn in much greater detail and quite obviously intended to represent Janice's actual face. It was the shape of a human face—larger at the forehead, narrowing at the chin—complete with eye-shaped eyes, lips, cheekbones, forehead wrinkles, and long wavy, black hair. What was most frightening about the face was the mouth, which was wide open. And the teeth were showing, and they were crooked and misshapen and sharp. All of them. Sharp. And atop the head were two horns, like those belonging to the devil—or Dracula, I thought, in his most monstrous form. And beneath this second face—which was both Janice's face and the devil's—was written: no medication.

When I got back to bed, I looked at Janice but, in the dark, all I could see was the cartoon version of her face. Horns and teeth and all. I turned my head away and pressed my face down into the mattress. The wind was blowing.

17

Everywhere looked like autumn but felt like summer. The leaves were brown and orange and falling, but the temperature was the same as it had been—hotter even. School had started, and I saw more and more students passing by my window, whichever way, keeping their heads down as they went.

The renewed fight against ISIS in Syria, a U.N. warning about climate change, a destructive earthquake in Albania, a woman in Texas found dead on her way to work was killed by multiple feral hogs, more germs than you realize in your kitchen.

On the internet: another presidential debate. One candidate explained his proposal for universal basic income. The total automation of labor, he was saying, is inevitable. In ten years, eighty percent of the American workforce will be phased out of existence. There won't be jobs left in the service industry or the manufacturing industry, which will soon be accomplished by machines. Candidate K, in response, claimed that, in fact, the industries of contraction and labor were alive and well. He argued that in a few years, construction companies will be undermanned and, therefore, in desperate need of a new, young workforce. This need will produce in-demand, high-paying jobs. Our future will be built on hard work.

With Janice there was more sex, and the more sex there was the more it felt like sex. We saw each other three days a week—Sunday, Monday, Wednesday. Those were called "my days." I didn't ask about the other days, or whose days they were. I was happy to have my own. Three was enough for me, and three was enough for Janice, too, because, as she put it, she didn't want our relationship to interfere with her life. I don't want our sex to distract me from my own time, she had said. Plus, she added. I have other obligations, social and romantic. Other people, too. It's not just you and me, she said. There's always a third party. There's a whole world to experience.

We emailed each other photos and YouTube videos and songs of Spotify. We met at the bookstore. We went to the cafe and the bar and the theater. We drank. We walked. We took the side streets. The weather was fine. Time passed, but I couldn't feel it. A line turned into a loop, a loop into a circle. We ended up in the same place we started. Nowhere in particular. We went to the grocery store and the bike shop and the bagel joint and the bakery. Mostly Janice talked and I listened. *Furthermore, moreover, additionally, what's more, therefore, thus, thusly, and so on.* Art, sex, and the proletariat. Aesthetics and perversion. Sex and Art. Ethics and the proletariat and the pedophilic elite. I was Janice's convert, her would-be disciple. She was un-repressing me, she said. She was opening me up to a whole world of possible selves. She said: change your life. Be yourself, she said. Be your real self.

Each day was a din of voices and vibrations,

cars and trucks rumbling through the streets. The sky turned and turned, drained of color. It appeared and disappeared. The buildings sprawled out, lowly and thin. The yoga studio and the bag store and the public library. The light obliterated them. The power lines buzzed louder, and swarms of flies buzzed beneath them.

One day, we met at a narrow hotel in San Francisco—a sleazy place, cheap, the kind of hotel that offers an hourly rate—so we could have sex in front of the room's street-facing window.

We stood up when we did it. I was behind her, and she faced the glass, so that she could attract passersby, make eye contact with them. She said it was hot, and she liked the danger of it—the possibility of being caught. And it seemed like she wanted to be caught. She pressed her hands and face hard into the glass. She screamed, exaggeratedly, as if for help.

I contorted—pulled back the upper half of my body, cranking my neck away, and extended my lower half forward, cock and all, so as not to see or be seen. After a while, Janice turned around, wedged her back against the windowsill, pressed her body against the glass and spread out.

She wrapped her legs around me and looked down to watch me sliding in and out. I watched her watching it. She did not lift her head, not once. She fixated on the repetition and mechanisms of it.

It was exactly what I did and did not want.

Now he goes slower, she said, and I went slower. Now he goes faster.

When it was over, Janice thanked me for doing it. She reached over and plucked a loose hair off my bare arm and held up between her thumb and pointer, as if making a benediction, to show me.

Don't you want to know if anyone saw us?

I shrugged.

They did, she said. Lots of them.

•

Later, Janice and I were walking nowhere, wandering off the main roads, near the highway. The sun fell behind rows of incongruous apartment buildings. The sky lit up red and empty like a battle scene without soldiers to fight.

Do you think I'd like your novel? She said, apropos of nothing.

Not really.

Why not?

I don't know.

Is it one of those *lit bro* novels?

What's a lit bro novel?

Is it about a sad man who feels sorry for himself? Is it one of the huge books that wants to impose a phallic vision onto the world? Are you one of those *dude* writers who only describes women's tits?

I hope not.

Janice put her hands in her pockets and jingled some keys or coins. She faced forward, looking out there, ahead of us, with exerted effort. She squinted, and opened her eyes and squinted again, as if trying to see something far away. I looked out there too but saw nothing. A thin complex that cut diagonally from the north, run-down houses, patchy lawns, rotting wood, some windows barred and boarded-up.

So, why wouldn't I like it? It's too philosophical, or what?

Yeah, maybe.

Why are you writing it?

I can't help what I write or don't write.

What's it about?

Nothing.

Tell me, she said.

It's long, I said, trying to avoid summarizing another novel I wasn't writing. I glanced down at my wristwatch as if to suggest we didn't have time for me to tell it.

Give me the pitch, she said. Go.

Okay. I decided to take this as an opportunity to impress Janice, maybe, so I made something up. A story. A long one. The longest yet. It took half an hour to tell. It went something like this:

There's this guy, Gad is his name, who, when the novel begins, is married to the love of his life. A woman, Bobbi. He calls her Bob, and sometimes Robert, Bobert, Bobber, or Bo. Both are somewhere in their late thirties. They've been married for—I don't know—seven years. Maybe more. They live in Brooklyn.

Gad is a large man and has cultivated what he considers to be a historically masculine look—worn-out jeans and flannel shirts and boots. He wears a large beard. Bobbi also dresses like a man—she wears more or less the same outfits as Gad. Sometimes, they even share clothes.

She has red hair and, each morning, meticulously places it into a messy bun, giving off a blasé look. Gad and Bobbi are both novelists. Gad has not been able to write because, as he puts it, he wants to write something original, to imagine or invent something out of thin air. He wants to tell an old story in a new way, or a new story in an old way. Old—as old as the Greeks and Children of Israel and older, as old as war, as grand as mythology. But every story he tells is wrong—every story gets something wrong. Each story, in its own way, tells a lie. It's a trap, he thinks.

Eventually, Gad decides that he must simply tell his own story and no one else's—the only story he's allowed to tell. Not an invention, but a confession. But the problem is this. He has no story of his own—nothing to confess. His life, so far, is boring, mostly, or at least uneventful. So far.

Bobbi, by contrast, writes with ease. Plus, she's brilliant and charismatic. Up to this point, Bobbi has been very secretive about her writing. She has not, on principle, allowed Gad to read any of it.

You can read it when it's published, she says.

So, Gad—who does not push back—waits. Her first novel is published to great acclaim. Her novel explores sex, sexuality and all that. Some reviewers even call the novel "high erotica," or "pornographic art." One critic writes that Bobbi's novel "pushes the boundaries of what is considered acceptable for the average reader of literary fiction."

Gad finally reads it.

It goes without saying, Gad is happy for Bobbi. He's excited for his wife, but—like many readers of his generation, or, maybe, many readers in general—he assumes that Bobbi's novel is autobiographical. He assumes, too, that the primary love interest in the novel, whose name is Red, is modeled after himself, Gad. And indeed, Gad recognizes himself in Red: his muscular build, weightlifting schedule, gambling habits, drinking preferences, even his idiosyncratic colloquialisms. He says things, for example—"el" instead of "the," and "four shores" instead of "for sure." Red resembles Gad in other ways, too. He wears a dad hat—a plain, shallow, beige cap that sits loosely atop his head, always about to fall off.

Towards the middle of Bobbi's novel, however, during the first full-length sex scene, Gad fails for the first time to recognize himself in Red. Here Gad encounters a long description of Red's penis, that is—surely, definitely, he thinks—not his own penis. The description goes like this: *The piece was paunchy and plump. A short, stalky motherfucker, weirdly compressed, flattened even—a condensed baguette, a smashed-down soda can. And when it hardened, it extended not upward, but out, so that it grew in width. So broad it was that, when I tried—and I tried hard, very hard, in truth—I could not put my mouth around it, and it was of no use to me.*

Gad feels confused not only because he does

not recognize the penis, but also because he wonders whether a) he has deluded himself about the nature of his own penis, and b) the described penis is another man's penis, and, if so, whose?

He removes his pants, then and there, to examine, naked from the waist down, his own penis, and sure enough: no. His penis is perfectly normal. Too normal. If anything, his penis is the opposite of the one described. It is long and thin and unremarkable.

It's just fiction, Gad. It's all made-up. He laughs at himself. He forces himself to laugh, and he laughs so loudly that, when he hears himself laughing, he does not recognize his laughter, and the sheer volume of it exposes the laugh as false. The laugh, he thinks, resembles a moan—a howl, a sob. And when Gad becomes aware that his laugh sounds like a sob, he begins, in fact, to cry—to weep hysterically.

Days pass and months. Gad can't move past it, can't get over that description, that pancake penis, the widening of it, can't forget his own fears and insecurities and fragilities. He believes—or he wants to believe—that he's being irrational and moody. That the narrator isn't Bobbi, anyway. Fool.

But he can't let go, and slowly it eats away at his brain. He can't get the image out of his head—the fat cock, the cartoonish girth of it. He sees visions of his wife trying to fit her tiny mouth around it. He sees that image when he goes to bed, when he wakes up, and—worst of all—when he himself tries to have sex with Bobbi with his average penis. Pencil dick.

Gad begins to suspect that Bobbi is or was—whether now or at the time of writing her novel—cheating on him with another man. Suspicion turns into sorrow, and sorrow into anger, anger into loathing, loathing into confusion, confusion into impotence. His sex performance worsens, and Bobbi notices that he isn't himself—that he hasn't been himself for a long time. She suspects that he is jealous—not of some imaginary lover, but of her literary success. After all, it's obvious: Gad, in his anger and confusion and impotence, has not been writing.

How could he write?

Eventually Gad's paranoia turns into a self-fulfilling prophecy. Bobbi does begin an affair. One and then another. Soon Bobbi can't stand to be around Gad—not only because he mopes and broods around the house, but because she correlates his moodiness with her writerly success. And so, in a fit of misunderstanding and irony, propelled by her feminist convictions, Bobbi files for divorce.

Gad tries to defend himself, tries to explain his actions and salvage what might be left of the marriage, but Bobbi—who interprets Gad's insecurities as insults, and his confessions as attempts at manipulation—rejects all of it.

Nothing can be done. It's no one's fault—or, probably, it's Gad's fault, and he knows it, and that's what hurts.

Now he is alone. He borrows some money from his parents and moves into a small studio apartment with a shared kitchen. I finally have something to write about, he thinks, I finally have a story to tell. A quiet story about divorce. It will make a good excerpt, he thinks, for *The New Yorker*.

Here he goes. Gad sets out to write an auto-fictional revenge novel that will indeed do everything Bobbi had accused him of doing in the first place—it will shame and humiliate and vilify her, his wife.

Look at him writing. He writes and, for a while, his writing is good. He works day and night. The writing consumes his life, and his life becomes his writing. He sets goals and deadlines, and he meets them.

In his novel (which is inside my novel), he describes Bobbi the way she had described him: stubborn, belligerent, dictatorial, brash.

Soon Gad reaches the end of his novel, and it's here that he burns out. He stalls. He feels himself either overworked by his writing or bored with it. He doesn't know how to end it. Does it end with the divorce? Does it end with the beginning of writing the novel itself? No. No, there is no resolution there, no intrigue. There is neither coldness nor heat. Does it end with Gad alone, as he is now? With Gad as himself, dejected and sad, drinking toward sleep? Toward death? No, there is no catharsis in the pathetic. No epiphany in self-loathing. No. The story must be true. True as possible.

Days pass, every one identical to the one before it. His shower is the same every time he takes it. Lukewarm.

One night at a bar, Gad, who sits alone on a barstool, his shoulders slumped, is approached by a man named Blue. Blue is the man's surname, of course, though he does not reveal his first name. Blue's a casual guy, neither big nor small, neither handsome nor ugly. He speaks slowly and in a low register. His voice is low and raspy and gritty. Says words like "nary" and "your'n" and "nuh-huh." Gad likes this about him, and he feels instantly bonded to the man. He trusts him. The two men connect and converse about sports and construction projects on the east bridge and the New Jersey turnpike, and the weather, and how crowded the city gets this time of year with tourists. They express a mutual disdain for politics and politicians. Fucking crooks, Blue says. Shitbag criminals.

Now Gad is enlivened enough to admit that he's a writer, that he's writing a novel about his life and his divorce, about his ex-wife Bobbi who wrote a novel about him and got it all wrong and might have ruined his reputation forever.

A revenge novel, said Blue. Huh. Never heard of that before.

But I have a problem, says Gad. I can't finish it and I don't know why. It's not coming to me. How to end a story which is your own life, a life which, you hope, will continue after the story of it is told?

Blue thinks about that.

Do I end on a minor or major key? An image? An epiphany? A symbolic rebirth? A symbolic death? A literal one?

Blue is thinking.

I haven't had an epiphany, Gad says, so, I can't write one. Do I wait until my life presents an ending? Do I simply end abruptly, here and now? I don't know. Maybe it's this city. It gets in my head, and it's hard to see beyond it.

Just then, Blue sits up straight and turns to look Gad in the face. Listen, he says. Listen, brother. I own a house, a getaway pad. A bit of a vacation home, you could call it. It's very far away from here, in another world practically. You could go there and finish your novel, clear your head a bit and think. Shit, you could go there for the entire season, if you need it.

Gad is dumbfounded, speechless with gratitude.

Blue claps his hands. It's in the southwest, he says. In the desert. Southern New Mexico, near the border. Las Cruces, a barren place. You could go this winter and stay as long as it takes you to finish it.

For hours, the two men hash out the details. Gad will finish teaching his courses, and as soon as the semester is over, he'll drive across the country, and stay at Blue's house until he finishes the novel, or until the novel—he jokes—finishes him.

For several weeks, Gad and Blue exchange a few emails, mostly to swap logistical information—Blue describes the house to Gad. It's stucco, he says, the color of sand. It has a red door. A tin roof. Garage. Concrete wall. Path with stones. And it has a giant window that overlooks nothing. He tells him that there is a key taped to the bottom of an empty pot on the left side of the house, in the backyard, behind the gate.

Weeks later, Gad is on the road. He drives for three days—I-70 to I-44 to I-20 to Whitehorse Lane, to Crimson Avenue.

He stops to sleep and eat breakfast in Indianapolis and Tulsa, stays in motels as cheap as he can find, the kind of places people go to cheat on their spouses. He wakes and eats the continental breakfast—packaged pies and muffins.

And he keeps driving and never stays too long at any one pitstop, rarely stops to use the bathroom (he pees in a Gatorade bottle).

He's going west, now southwest, now south. Suddenly he's in the desert, though he had not seen it coming—though it came without warning. The sun follows him until it falls into the foreground and sits on the horizon. It turns the black road pale, impossible to see; and the road extends downward and drops into a hellish panorama. He drives through one small town and then another, past thin houses, dilapidated strip malls, sun-burnt boneyards with rusted trucks and broken-down machinery, concrete schools with empty playgrounds and deteriorated swing sets and shallow dirt pits.

When he arrives, the stars flood the desert floor. But there is this problem: now, here, at this address, the point to which Google Maps has guided him, does not exist. There is no house. No number 185 Crimson. Only an empty plot. A patch of gravel the size of a small parking lot—wild, uncleared sagebrush and rock.

He conjures up the personality traits most stereotypical to his self-image: toughness, composure. But beneath the skin, maybe on its surface, he feels terror coursing through himself, pulsing through his veins. He's lost, irritated, nowhere near his intended destination.

He checks his phone. No service.

He jumps back into his car and slams the door and starts the engine and hits the gas and drives back, away, to find whether he had made a wrong turn. He turns back along the route he came, seeking out a side road, a secondary path, a fire road maybe, a private driveway. He re-enters the house address but, without service, the machine is unable to trace another way. He goes through the night and the stars cast a dense and filmy light like gossamer and lace. He drives back into town—barely a town, barely a village even, even smaller, and totally dark. Still, he cannot pick up a signal. No service, no sign.

He drives on and on, and in the desert outside of town, he does find a few houses, but none is right. None matches Blue's description.

Gad's fear turns into fatigue and fatigue turns into listlessness and indifference, and eventually, as the sun begins to rise, he pulls his truck over there, on the side of a road—which is no real road, a wide line cut in the dirt— he stretches himself across the bench seat, and tucks his backpack beneath his head, and sleeps and does not dream.

In the afternoon, the desert flares up and he sees everything: the expanse of nothing—and the whole world seems to lose its meaning, its purpose, if it ever had one.

He turns on the car, and rolls down the windows, and rummages through his backpack until he finds a granola bar and half a bag of trail mix. Then he resumes his search.

Hours of driving, circles within circles. He sees the same hills, same dry ravines—cacti and sage and rocks. He's losing his sense of direction now, looking more and more at his phone, helpless and frustrated. His frustration causes him to resent Bobbi again, to hate her again, to hate her in a way that he had not hated her before.

The sun is pale and white. Gad wonders whether this—here, right now—is how his novel will end.

His phone reads five o'clock now and he's running out of gas. He makes his way back into town—not really a town—and fills up at a Texaco and heads to a diner for some real food and maybe some coffee.

The diner is empty, save one gray couple sitting in the back booth. The decor is modeled white and pink—a fleshy pink, like the skin of a naked rat. The floor is tile, a pink and white checkered pattern. The chairs have overstuffed seats and backrests. Flesh everywhere. Gad sits in a booth, but the seat is unusually wide, longer than the length of his thigh, so that, when sits against the back of the booth, his legs strain to reach the ground, and the tables are unnaturally high so that he must lift his elbows above his nipples to rest set them down and he feels like a child.

He stands and moves to the bar.

The waiter emerges from the kitchen.

He orders a cobb salad and fries and coffee. She nods and walks away and returns with a plastic cup of water. He downs the cup in a single effort.

The waiter observes him, looks him up and down. She's gaunt, tall and thin and worn-out. Passing though?

Sorry?

Passing through, she says again.

I'm looking for a house, he says. I'm going to be living here for a while, going to stay for the season. But I can't find it. I'm lost.

She shows her teeth. What's the address?

He hesitates, skeptical of her motivations, but then decides he has, now, nothing to lose. He holds up his phone on which is written: 185 Crimson.

She shrugs. Tony, yells the waitress. Tony!

A large man emerges from the kitchen—a man who resembles Gad in size and appearance, though his beard is bigger and uncombed and yellowing around the mouth. Maybe he's the cook? The manager?

Tony, says the waitress. You know a Crimson around here? Crimson road?

Gad holds out his phone so that Tony can see it. Tony squints at the machine and flicks his tongue. There's no Crimson here, he says. Not in this town.

Am I in the wrong town?

Dunno, he says. No Crimson, though. I know that. There is a Simpson Ave and a Christen

Ave. But I doubt that's what you're after.

Gad frowns, why's that?

Dunno. But those roads are far off. Out of town. It's wack out there. Drug houses and such.

Gad nods and thanks them. He eats his meal as fast as he can. Drinks his coffee, and leaves.

He enters the new roads into his phone. The machine's map locates a 185 Christen, and Gad is gone, back on the road. He's driving with a new purpose now, faster and with a sense of urgency. The tires screech and howl against the uneven asphalt. The asphalt turns to gravel, and gravel to dust. The dust jumps up and makes a cloud around the truck.

Now he sees in the distance by the last light of sunset, on the crown of a small bluff, a house. The house is Blue's. It looks exactly as it had been described. Single story, the color of sand, stucco, tin roof, with a single car garage. A short concrete wall surrounds the property, and a thin path outlined with thin stones leads up from the driveway to the front door. The front door is as Blue had said it would be. Red.

And the house has that giant window, too, overlooking nothing.

But even as Gad begins to experience that long-awaited sense of relief, he feels also dread; for in that large window there is a light on, and in that driveway, there is a car—a station wagon—and that red door, look, it is slightly ajar.

Gad pulls up to the house anyway and, after sitting in the car for several minutes and—confused, lacking the energy to make any other decision—convinces himself everything's fine. The light was left on by mistake, surely. The car is always there, right, right. The door is not open, but only seemed to be so. He steps out of the car and approaches the house. He prepares himself for whatever awaits him inside. He clenches his fists. He removes his knife, and puts it in his back pocket where, if necessary, he can reach it again.

Turns out, everything is fine.

The door is locked, and no one is inside. Gad finds the key and enters.

The interior of the house looks like it's underwater. It gives him the feeling of swimming, struggling to catch his breath. The walls are painted a weird blue, almost green, and the carpet is blue too, though much darker in tone, and the windows are dark, though the color is difficult to determine, and when the starlight shines through, they look blue, black, gray. The house is full of potted plants and cacti and framed paintings of the desert, constant reminders of what is still there, right outside, surrounding the house. There are also three large paintings of the house itself, but at different times of day.

Gad breathes. He's starting to calm down. To relax. He's trying. He removes a bottle of whiskey from his backpack and sips from the bottle. Most of the cupboards in the kitchen are empty, but he finds a collection of glassware in one of the drawers. He pulls out a tumbler, and rinses it out in the sink, and sets it on the counter, and fills it to the rim with whiskey. Then he sips from the bottle and sets it on the kitchen table—a worn and pale and thin table on which rests an empty glass bowl. He tries to watch a film on the laptop, but the house has no internet. No internet and no cellphone service. He downs his glass of whiskey and pours another. He paces around the living room. The drink is hard to swallow—feels like he's drowning in it. He takes out his notebook and begins to write. Nothing. Nothing again.

That night, Gad orbits sleep, but never enters it. He remains in a dream-like state of agitation and half-consciousness, at once with himself, and with someone else. He tosses and turns and floats around the room. There is an image he cannot see. A face appears in the window. The shape of a human body in the folds of the curtain.

Now his body senses movement outside the house. He hears the rushing of a train passing. The room shakes and quivers. The moonlight falls through the window and fills the room. His phone, when he looks at it, reads 3:30.

It's late enough to rise, he thinks. To rise and begin to work.

He sits up, and his eyes are drawn to the doorframe—now outlined by a sharp light on the other side.

Had he forgotten to turn off the lights?

Now he's wide awake. Now he's up and moving. After putting on his clothes, Gad unsheathes his knife and tucks it into his back pocket. Then, still trembling, he removes the blade and clutches it with his good hand. He opens the door slowly and walks into the living room and hears someone muttering a private language. The ramblings of a madman. The voice is a familiar one, deep and gritty.

When Gad turns the corner, Blue is there. He sits. He drinks a dark liquid. He's almost completely naked—he wears nothing but a pair of old gym shorts and tube socks pulled up to the middle of his shins. He holds a large hunting knife with an orange handle and a serrated blade.

Gad staggers and halts at the bright light. What are you drinking? he says, though it was not the question he meant to ask.

Blue seems not to recognize Gad. He twitches. He jumps up and stumbles backward and bends his knees. Who the fuck are you? He's yelling now. Fuck, fuck. What are you doing in my house!

Gad steps back and crouches. You're drunk, he says.

Blue crouches too, as if to engage in some bizarre and exaggerated choreography. He raises his arms and swings the knife in the air to the right and the left and makes a jabbing motion with it. Get out of my house. Get the fuck out.

Gad's voice is quivering, and he struggles to spit out the words. It's me. Don't you remember? You told me I could stay here. I'm here to finish my novel, remember?

Blue swings his knife again and lowers his body to stabilize his stance.

Gad stutters, trying to reason with Blue—to explain who he is, and why he's there. He recounts the narrative of his novel. Don't you remember? I came here to write the ending, he says.

To finish the story.

Blue sways and wobbles a little and grins to show his teeth and laughs with his mouth open in a way that indicates both courage and fear. He steps forward.

Gad steps back. He holds his knife up in the air to match his.

And just then, in the exchange between them, Gad sees something in Blue, something he might not have noticed had the circumstances not been so strange. He sees that Blue is not quite smiling, not grinning exactly, but smirking—the corner of his lip curls up just so. It exudes deliberation and craft.

This is it. This is how my novel will end. Of course, Blue remembers me. He must remember. And if he does remember, then, here and now, he is offering me an opportunity to end. The situation is contrived, fictional, but its outcomes, its consequences are true. The stakes are real. Bloodshed or cowardice. Anything else is unbelievable. No one would believe this, and so Blue is—he must be— staging reality for my sake.

This is how the novel ends.

Gad draws his knife. This is his chance to win his life back. To reclaim what he believed he'd lost—his dignity, his self-worth, his art.

What should he do?

Maybe he runs out to his car and drives away, leaving behind all his belongings—his clothes and his computer and his notebook. Maybe he drops to his knees and begs Blue to let him go. Maybe he asks, gently as he can, to gather his possessions. Maybe he promises to leave in peace, says: this has all been a mistake. Maybe Blue lets him go, maybe not. Maybe he fights. Maybe he wins, maybe loses. Maybe they wrestle brutally— symbolic of strife and war and glory and defeat, microcosmic of our struggle with God and angels and demons and death and all that, reduced to a meaningless game, an encounter between two men the rest of the world remains indifferent to.

•

When I finished my story, Janice stopped and made a thinking face, and then began to walk again. Then she stopped walking again and stepped back and looked down, up. I understand, she said.

Understand what?

Your story, she said. Your long story. You are a storyteller. You don't speak much unless you're telling your stories. But I understand what you mean.

I don't understand.

It's an allegory, she said. Gad is an observer in his own life. A tourist or a consumer inside it. And what he consumes is experience. But he wants a bigger narrative.

Maybe.

But the problem is that narratives are dead, she said. That's what Gad's book is about, isn't it? The existential fatigue of stories. Gad tries to turn his life into a story—he lives out a plot of adventure. A quest narrative.

Now Janice paused and looked at me, as if suddenly recognizing a stranger. Her face lit up. Big eyes.

Now, she said, I know why you joined our community. This is why you're here, why you joined our community. To reclaim the narrative. She laughed.

I wanted to tell her that I didn't know anything about her community, but I was afraid of how she might react; and I wanted to tell that I had pulled Gad's Book out of my ass, that it meant—as far as I could say—nothing to me.

Gad wants intensity and adventure and violence.

Violence? No. That's not it at all.

It's true what they say. The poet does not know from whence he speaks, dude. You cannot hear what your own story is saying.

It's just a story.

Everyone wants violence at some point in their lives, real violence. Real violence is a necessity, a lifeblood. And that's the decision Gad must make.

I had a feeling like I needed to take a shower.

Violence is how we reclaim our reality, she said. Our narrative.

Now the sun was set and the streetlights clicked and darkness came on.

You're going to the protest tomorrow, right? she asked in a way that indicated I was supposed to know what she was talking about.

The protest.

The protest, yeah. I think you should come.

She looked at me and leaned in as if to kiss me but did not. Her eyes were deep-set and dark. I could see a glossy version of myself there, contained and shrunken down. She smelled like something familiar. Something simple. Dirt. She smelled like dirt. Not soil or soot or loam, no—not the smell of dirt. More like dust. Or not dust, but sand. Dry and grainy sand. The sand at the bottom of the ocean. Desert sand.

I could taste it.

And I said yes. Yes, I said, just like that. I'll be there.

18

Next day Janice showed up in black—black jeans and a Fall Out Boy t-shirt.

You listen to that crap?

Crap?

I pointed to her shirt.

She looked down. This? This's Julio's. It's all I have that's black. She looked at me. Why aren't you wearing black?

•

I didn't want to arrive too soon—didn't want to spend any time at the protest before the protest began. I walked slowly, slower than walking, and feigned interest in the shops on Telegraph, pretending to investigate windows. I pointed at a row of pewter miniatures: wizards, trolls, skulls, and soldiers. Look at this, I said.

She looked.

And look at this. I pointed to a mural painted on a narrow door between two brick buildings. The scene depicted a man trapped inside a shower. The shower head squirted out cartoonishly large drops of water. Was it water? He was fully clothed, the man—shoes, socks, suit and tie. He wore glasses. He held himself up precariously in the tight space—his legs pushed up against one wall, and his hands pressed against the other to keep his feet off the ground. He contorted his body away from the running water to keep himself dry. The situation was absurd and inconsequential and ridiculous. I'd seen the mural hundreds of times. I'd walked past it nearly every day, going one direction or the other, and yet, I hadn't regarded it until now. I hadn't thought about it until I pretended to think about it.

I said, you'd think he could just reach out and turn the shower off, right? See, there's the knob. I pointed. Why doesn't he turn it off? The knob's right there. Maybe he can't see it. Maybe it doesn't work. Or maybe, for some reason, he doesn't want to do it.

Janice was looking down at her phone smiling at whatever she was seeing on the screen.

•

The sidewalks on campus were covered in chalk drawings, peace and love signs, suns and flowers, trees and stick figures holding hands and coffee cups and heart-shapes. It was written *nobody tells the truth, vote for nobody, nobody for president, we are nobody.* Someone else wrote *hope for hope for hope.*

We wandered among the mob of protesters or counter-protestors. The mob grew. It spilled over the public square and into the walkways and the terraces and grass plots. Many protesters were, as before, outfitted in the garbs of anonymity: black pants, hoodies, masks, bandanas, and brand name jackets. Columbia, North Face and Nike. Biker helmets and paintball helmets and snorkeling goggles and aviator sunglasses. Sports gear, too. Yankees, Real Madrid, Steelers, Pirates, Penguins. A rise and fall of bodies—a singular body swaying in all directions, bounding and flowing, loud and louder, waiting for the protest to begin.

They marched in circles and chanted their mantras and slogans—banners, posters, flags bounded up and down, rippling lightly in the vague sea breeze.

Just then, I was called. Someone called my name.

I saw him: a menacing figure dressed in a single black jump suit and a scream mask. Ten or twelve stood around him, almost a complete circle, as if performing a ritual. Some of them nodded. Some watched stoically—they seemed to watch, sizing us up—behind their enormous sunglasses and masks. We walked closer.

And that's when I saw him. The man.

He pulled off his mask so that it sat on top of his head. I recognized him immediately. It was him. From the bookstore. Ezekiel. There he was, making a face like he wanted to have sex. He huffed and hiccuped and seemed out of breath. Man, he said. I remember you. From the book-store.

Janice looked at each of us in turn. You know each other?

From the bookstore, I said. Yeah.

We all shook hands—hi, hi, good to see you, what a coincidence, etc.

It was a crippling awkwardness. There was too much to think about and thinking, in that loud place, was hard to do. Was Zeke Janice's partner?

Zeke kept looking at me, up, down. Where is your uniform? he said. Where is your black?

I looked down at myself to see what I was wearing. Jeans and a dark green over shirt. I forgot, I lied. I just forgot. I ran my hands down my chest and grabbed my shirt by the hem and tugged it, as if to show how the shirt was good. Good enough.

Janice poked me in the chest. I tried to tell him, she said.

Zeke put his mask back on. This isn't going to work, he said. That's not our look, you look like an outsider. We don't know what's going to happen and trust me, you don't want anyone to be able to identify you.

The crowd was getting larger—larger and more restless. Police officers, carrying shields, wearing helmets, rode bikes toward the front of the group.

I have some extra clothes in my backpack, he said. Non-identifying.

Maybe I should go home, I said.

Zeke gestured for me to follow him. You can change in the bathroom, he said.

It's fine, I said. Really, I don't care.

Before I could refuse again, Zeke grabbed Janice's hand, and Janice grabbed mine, and we pushed our way through the compact crowd into the student union, packed in with protestors. Body heat and forearms and foreheads and fists. Animalistic grunts, groans, and exhalations. We went into the gender-neutral bathroom. Janice waited

155

outside. Zeke elbowed his way through the long line of people waiting to use the stalls, and the even longer line for the urinals. He stopped on the far end of the sinks and turned to face the crowd. Sorry, he said to no one in particular. We're not here for the toilet, we just need to change into new clothes. He pulled his mask up again and opened his backpack and took out from it a pair of black sweatpants and a black apron. Put these on, he said.

Now? Right here?

Yes, he said. We don't have time to wait for a stall. Do it here.

What are these? They smell terrible.

My work clothes, he said.

I held the sweatpants up by the waist. What work?

I'm a butcher.

You butcher meat in this? I can't wear these. Look at them. They're enormous.

Just tighten the drawstring and roll up the legs, he said. It doesn't matter what you look like. It only matters that you look like no one.

I'll look like a child, I said. I'll be easy to identify like that. The child, that's what people will say. Look at that child.

A child among children! he said and held out his backpack and shook it and pulled it open. Here. You can put your clothes in here.

I took off my shirt, button by button. I worked my way down. As I began to unfasten my belt, I suddenly remembered: underwear, I wasn't wearing any. I froze.

I wanted my eyes to disappear.

Zeke shook the bag in front of my face and stomped his foot and looked over his shoulder. Why'd you stop? he said. Hurry.

Can you hold up a towel or something? What else do you have in that bag?

Nothing, man. Just hurry. No one cares about your body.

I clenched my jaw and put on the long-sleeve shirt and threw the apron around my neck and tied a knot with the straps together at the back. It was huge—the bib hung past my knees. It fit like a nightgown or a rain poncho—a Halloween costume of a butcher.

I leaned farther forward, hunched lower, causing the bib to drape down, and I undid my belt and let my pants fall to the floor. Zeke watched, as if to monitor my progress, or ensure I fulfilled his orders. I surveyed the crowd in my peripheral vision, to see whether anyone else was looking at me. Everyone was. An entire group of strangers, their identities safely masked, watched me undress until naked.

I felt hot and cold intermittently, and I squirmed and struggled to pull Zeke's sweatpants around my waist. I pulled tight the draw string and folded the waistband into itself, and I rolled up the legs three times in loose folds that bunched around my ankles.

I stood up and looked around and gave Zeke the thumbs up, and he put his hand on my shoulder and held me still. Wait, he said. He handed me a pair of aviator sunglasses. Put these on.

You're kidding, I said.

He wasn't kidding.

I put them on and looked at myself in the mirror. I resembled a child wearing his father's outfit—pretending to be an adult in oversized work clothes.

I waddled toward the exit, all suited up.

Janice looked up from her phone and saw me and laughed hard through her nose. Zeke reached into his bag again, pulled out a black bandanna and gave it to Janice. Here. This is for you. Here.

Janice put the bandanna over her mouth and handed me her phone. Let's take a selfie, she said. And we did.

While he was talking to someone else, I turned to Janice and mouthed the words: Who is this guy?

What? Janice yelled.

I grabbed her shoulder. Who is this guy?

Zeke? She smiled. He's crazy.

Is he your partner? I asked.

What?

Is he your partner?

She must have misunderstood me because she simply repeated herself. He's crazy, she said. Totally crazy.

She said it like it was a good thing.

•

The sun had set, and new moonlight fell on the black bloc. A deluge of shadows descending over the structures of academia. Signs and banners led the way, followed by a slew of disembodied arms waving their phones in the air, taking videos and shining flashlights. Several photographers and cameramen stood outside the mass, and each time one of them tried to follow, or infiltrate, they were held off, pushed back.

Someone said, don't let that fucking photographer in.

There's a plan, Zeke was telling me now, rally together at Sather Gate, chant and confront the enemy, the non-protestors, counter-protestors, the police.

And then what?

Then we march into campus toward the Sproul Plaza, where we'll shut down the event. We'll barricade the doors. Won't let anyone inside. Won't let them speak. By any means necessary.

We were in the middle of the crowd, tossed here and there by the gyrations of the mass, bodies on all sides. Someone toward the front of the crowd lit a flare—the kind you see on the side of the highway at night, surrounding an accident—that threw up a distressed signal into the sky and everything was red.

Zeke again reached into his backpack, and removed a plastic water bottle, half-empty with a clear, thick liquid, around which was a strip of duct tape and the letters L-A-W written in black. Hold this, he said.

I held it. What is it?

Antacid and water.

I stepped back. Is this a bomb?

Zeke showed his teeth. No, man. It's to repel pepper spray. If they get you, if they spray you, put this on your eyes. It'll help. He reached again into the bag—what seemed like an endless supply source—and removed a pair of weighted-knuckle gloves and slipped them on, the right and then the left, He clenched his fists and the gloves stretched and formed around his knuckles, and he fixed his eyes forward and started chanting. He pulled his mask down over his face and his voice became muffled.

What are you going to do with those?

He didn't answer but went on chanting.

We marched.

Zeke's clothes consumed me and concealed every contour of my body. They caused me to feel anonymous even to myself. I was small, smaller than usual. But the uniform gave me an authentic and genuine feeling. I was there, present.

Zeke went, We can't give the police a monopoly on violence!

I nodded and looked over at Janice, who walked stride for stride with Zeke on his right side. She was chanting, too. She had a lightness, a spring in her step that distinguished her from the other protestors.

Tighten up! Someone yelled from the back.

How could we be tighter? But we did get tighter. We were. We closed in, closer together, skin on skin, pressing into a single body as if by some outside strength. Then something started to happen at the front—a conflux, a clash.

From the front: Stick together!

From the back: Stand your ground!

Now people threw down their street signs. As some protesters moved laterally, one way or the other, the crowd was loosening up. Now it became less aimed and organized and more oblique, moving crabwise and flanking outward—off the sidewalks and the pathways. I moved with them, by them, and saw the cause of the sidelong reaction—policemen in full riot gear formed a line lengthwise, locking their bikes together to barricade the main pathway like Roman Legionnaires. The crowd, now thinner at the front, pushed back against the row of bikes, provoking police to push back. Don't do it, kid, said one officer, gripping his bike harder, resetting its upright position. Behind him, another police officer twirled his nightstick. He looked ahead, not at any one person, and seemed not to see anything at all.

Behind the row of cops was another group—much fewer in numbers than our own—of counter-protesters. Their faces were exposed, out in the open. They even seemed underdressed, animalistic, practically naked. They wore red hats and jorts and Fred Perry polos and t-shirts with the sleeves cut off.

The two crowds pushing toward the police officers, the only blockade between them. It was at this point—the point at which three distinctive bodies, each with a sense of righteousness and overconfidence—that the protest veered into a different kind of wave. A distinctive and pointed action. Us against others.

And now, almost immediately, there was a

change in tone, a collapse into an archaic contest. Two lanky hooded figures wrestled a bike from a police officer, freeing up his hands to reach for his nightstick. He pulled it from his belt and began to swing aimlessly at the crowd like a man hacking through brush. Several others swarmed the officer, causing him to stagger and sway and fall. I stumbled and moved out of the way. Two thieves carried the bike toward the back of the crowd. A few other cops ran to defend the now bike-less officer, flat on his back, from the sudden barrage of anonymous punches. Jab, jab, hook, jab. This caused the once-firm unit of armored authorities to sever, to break into clusters of two or three. Some officers teamed up to grab individual protesters. A police officer from the back of the unit: Get the fuck back! He threw a smoke bomb, which skidded along the ground in a semi-circle, popping like a firework, expelling red fog that swept across the scene, a cloud of haze and sightlessness obscured the already-obscure figures, obfuscating the outlines between things. I ran to the side, trying again to get out of the way. More smoke bombs. I was running in circles, avoiding contact with other people. The chanting turned incoherent, and the crowds intermingled and dispersed and scattered like the unweaving of a blanket, fraying in every direction. Some people ran away, some ran toward their opponents. It was awkward and ugly and primitive and blunt. Gang-up. Sucker punch. Cheap shot. Headlock. A swarm of undifferentiated bodies, arms and legs, writhing and pulling and dragging each other down. Every sound was a shout or an explosion, echoing and doubling over and blending into other eruptions and cries.

Someone yelled: *Get off the planet, you killed God!*

You killed God.

Now we are God.

I backpedaled and sidestepped and put my arms out to hold myself upright in the air. I looked around for Janice, but she was nowhere. Gone. I ran to look for her. Left and right. I ran back to where I was.

Zeke was easy to find. He was visibly personified, a whole heap of general rage. He was running, front to back, from one brawl to another. He swung and ran and swung again. He cried out. He moved nimbly like a trained fighter— light on his feet, throwing punches, quick jabs, without committing to any one specific scuffle. Then he vanished into a swarm of body parts, and I did not see him again. Behind me, I felt an intense heat on the back of my legs. Still backpedaling, I tripped and stumbled and turned around: the police officer's stolen bike was burning. Not more than ten feet from me. The flames billowed up and the smoke went up—like a sacrificial ceremony. One man punched another in the back of the head, who was, in turn, punched in the back of the head himself, and one threw a rock into a window, and a counter-protester hit him in the back with a stick, and one dropped a match into a trashcan, and the trashcan lit up like a face, and there was another broken window, and another, and the police were handcuffing people and throwing them to the ground, face-down, policemen everywhere with nightsticks and face shields and helmets, and another fire, an eruption of smoke that continued to ring and echo after the initial blast, and I looked and saw: the student union was burning—the flames and the shape of the flames twisted and turned up in the shape of the building they consumed, and smoke billowed out of the open windows and doors and unfolded again and again, doubling over and growing widthwise and laterally along the plane of vision: an eruption of smoke that continued to ring after the initial burst, burning and burned. People were running now, a horde, into and out of the smoke. It was almost impossible to tell who was on which side, and I was among them—running.

I remember punching someone. I hit him because he was there—right in front of me, where I happened to be going. And when he stood up, he hit me back. Right in the jaw. He was just a boy, a kid. Tall and hairless, head shaved, dark eyes. I saw him clearly. I would remember his face.

When I couldn't find Janice, I gave up. I ran away. I felt a certain clarity, true or not—a sudden ability to distinguish right from wrong. Everything was easy and light. Even as Zeke's clothing dragged me down, I kept running. Forward, away from the noise, holding the sweatpants up with one hand as I went.

When I was far enough from campus, I took off Zeke's apron and dropped it there, on the street, and I ran—down Bancroft and over and north on Shattuck, east on Allston, past the high school, then north, east on University, then south again, and farther south. I went until I couldn't feel my legs.

The night felt boundless around me, my ears still murmuring smoke and explosion.

Back home. I ran into my room. I got into bed. I covered my naked body in the sheets. My muscles tensed up and I felt a series of rhythmic contractions, a gentle current, building into a quickening pulse and then into a sudden unmissable release of pressure. The adrenaline rush was therapeutic. Briefly I lost all control of my senses, and felt like I was surrendering to some higher being.

PART THREE

19

The first novel I ever tried to write went like this.

A man—barely a man, not much older than a boy—moves to New York City to pursue what he imagines to be the writer's life. It's the life he has read about in magazine articles and novels and biographies about novelists.

In the beginning, he is a cliche of the idealistic artist type, driven to make art by the economy of modern feelings—anxiety, paranoia, compulsion. Eager to express the self as a way of being himself.

His first week in the city, he is consumed by the idea of it—the elusive and mythical labyrinth, the mysterious cityscape he encounters in films and paintings and books. He seeks novelty and immediacy, but remains vaguely exhausted, dogged by some unspeakable sense of unreality and routine. In Central Park, he thinks *Taxi Driver, Manhattan, Annie Hall, The French Connection, Serpico*. Looking up at the Empire State Building, he thinks: *The Godfather, American Psycho, Man on Wire*. In SoHo and Chelsea and Greenwich Village, he remembers Edward Hopper's "Nighthawks," "Night Windows," and "New York Office." He recounts the plots of *Invisible Man, Washington Square, Jazz, Great Jones Street, Money*. The whole city is dense and mapped and shot through with memory—not a blank page, but a page on which everything is already written.

He buys his groceries at Whole Foods, for example.

The man is Jed, short for Jedidiah. Jed needs money, so decides to quit writing—temporarily and with the faint belief that someday he will begin again.

He never does.

After a few weeks hunting, he takes a low-paying job as a copyeditor for manuscripts at a major publishing house, vetting manuscripts for a senior editor. How does he get this job? He knows someone who knows someone, that's how.

At first, Jed struggles to complete the basic requirements of his job. He reads manuscript after manuscript but cannot catch even the most apparent typo or grammatical error. He cannot see, for example, that from should be form, that lay should be lie. He makes almost no comments in the texts he reads.

And that's precisely his problem. He reads in all the ways that he should not: too close to the plot, too attached to characters and action. He is moved even by the most predictable stories: he weeps and laughs. He "suspends disbelief," as they used to say, and gives himself over to the magic, the illusion of a text.

He reads and thinks: This is what it means to be a person.

What does he mean by *this?*

Months pass. The weather changes.

One morning, an intern summons Jed into the office of his superior, who expresses dissatisfaction with his work performance.

I've seen your edits, he says. They're empty. Unmarked. Either you're not reading the manuscripts or you're not paying attention. Either you're lazy or you're bad. Either you're bad or you're naive. If you can't read more critically, says the superior, you're done. Your career in publishing is over.

Of course, the senior editor tells him all of this with the necessary degree of politeness, maintaining a passive-aggressive, pissed-off but technically delicate tone.

I read the stories carefully, Jed says. I enjoy reading.

You enjoy reading? So, you get distracted, you mean.

I love literature, says Jed.

The superior leans in and whispers now. You're not allowed just to love literature.

In time, Jed trains himself to read in different ways—to ignore the things which had brought him to the world of books in the first place. He localizes his reading, focusing his attention on individual words—words in themselves, words at the surface level. He does not think about irony, paradox, complexity, form, tone, meaning. He begins to understand everything literally. He learns to see only errors, scanning full manuscripts without reading them. Such is his concentration focused on the level of the word that, in time, he can scour entire documents without even noticing the events therein—words without language, grammar without writing, syntax without communication, character without context. A book, he thinks, is a vast field of objects under which have been buried an untold number of dead bodies. I must dig them up. I must cleanse the field of them.

Soon this becomes his life's greatest pleasure: to be a corrector, a proper user of words. To be the first person in his cohort to point out the failures of a given text. To add a missing apostrophe, to unsplice a comma. To change can't to cannot and *to* to *too*. He thinks, semicolon. He thinks, changes and change is. He thinks, who's and whose.

Now summer is over, and autumn is about to begin. Already the days are getting shorter. Jed has his thirty-three without anyone else around to celebrate with him.

When the publishing house promotes him to an editorial position, Jed decides to take a vacation to Europe. I don't know why he does it. He's always wanted to do it but previously lacked courage. Some readers might wonder: What makes him summon the courage now? Maybe he does because he is supposed to want it. Maybe he harbors a mimetic obsession with Europe and hopes to find there what he could not find in New York.

He decides to spend two weeks in Barcelona. Why Barcelona? Because he considers it both romantic and authentic. Both magical and real. Paris is too romantic, he thinks. Berlin is too real. Prague, too romantic. Brussels, too real. Rome is a cliché: too romantic. London is commercial and fake-feeling, and too much like New York. Also, too romantic. Unless you're in the southern part of London, in which case: too real. Madrid is boring. Lisbon is romantic. Dublin is real. Venice, romantic. Moscow, real.

He rents an Airbnb two blocks away from La Rambla Del Raval.

At first, his trip is uneventful and lonely. He wanders the city without direction, as he used to do in New York. He reads no books. He eats in dark restaurants lit by candlelight, and drinks until he's tired enough to sleep.

Many afternoons he sits alone in the pews of small churches. Not the cathedrals. Not the grand houses of God, but the inconspicuous and neglected shrines that God has never seen. The dark and empty ones, where no prayers are said.

One day, caught in a trance, he walks into a library and wanders up and down the long aisles, occasionally pausing to select a book and flip through its pages. He locates a copy of *Don Quixote*, he almost doesn't recognize it. He cracks the spine a few times, breaking it altogether in one place. He runs his fingers over the words, turns the pages deliberately, so they make a crisp clicking sound, and dogears some of the pages randomly. He has the desire to read it, but does not. He cannot.

A few days later, he meets a woman. He sees her at a cafe, hunched over an American publication of Roberto Bolaño's *2666*, which she holds loosely in one hand, letting the top of the book drop to the table, over and over, that makes a redundant, impatient tap. Appearing to use the novel as a prop, she frequently looks up to scan the room.

Jed approaches casually, en route to the bathroom, pretending not to notice her until that moment when he stands directly in front of her. He asks whether she happens to have an iPhone charger.

She doesn't.

Have you read the murder descriptions yet? he says. The Part About the Crimes?

I'm dead in the middle of it, she says. She drops the book on the table. Bolaño is a terrible writer, she says. He's all bad sentences. No style. And he's too academic. She flicks the cover of the book with her middle finger. One, two. Insufferable, she says.

He does not tell her that he finds her assessment of Bolaño to be itself too academic. He does not ask her to explain what's so academic about the depraved characters who inhabit the derelict landscapes of Bolaño's novels: lonesome gangsters, degenerate police officers, drugged-out detectives, apathetic scholars, impoverished poets, moralistic murders, schizophrenic sex workers.

The woman is Maggie—an American graduate student from Brown University studying literature. She has black hair and wears a blue and white striped long-sleeve shirt—typical of our idea of old sailors and painters in the 1940s and '50s. She carries a tiny backpack slung over one shoulder from which she produces a bottle of Vichy Catalan sparkling mineral water that looks like a tiny Gaudí building.

Turns out, she—like Jed—also reads books

174

to expose their underlying failures. Maybe she reads people this way, too.

For three consecutive days, they meet: drink coffee, go for walks, discuss books, music, culture, politics, the usual. Jed agrees with almost everything she says. Yes, he says. Yes.

But each day, around three o'clock, Maggie looks at her phone and tells Jed to go home. I need to work now, she says. I need you to leave.

Day four is Sunday. They eat ice cream and drink espresso. They ride bikes to the Picasso Museum, and, when faced with the ticket prices, decide that "once you've seen one Picasso, you've seen them all."

They ride to La Sagrada Familia just to take pictures from the outside. It looks like a giant spaceship, she says. He makes an alien face, but she accuses him of being a racist.

Later, they walk along the Platja de la Nova Icària. They drink more espresso. They drink beer. They drink more espresso. My body wants another ice cream, she says. They eat another ice cream. They do things lovers do, as in a cinematic montage. Then, slowly and without looking down, she reaches over to touch, only slightly at first, and then firmly later, his hand.

Briefly, he is happy. Maybe he's in love.

The sun sets and casts a long shadow over their faces, intensifying their expressions. He wants to kiss her but doesn't want to impose himself, doesn't want to play the stereotypical man, eager to get what he wants and fast. These thoughts inhibit him. He stiffens up.

This has been a perfect day, Maggie says, leaning into him.

She looks up and focuses her eyes on his lips, and he takes this as an invitation. He kisses her.

Only one thing is missing, she says.

What's that?

Love making, she says. That would make this a perfect day.

He thinks she has committed the cardinal sin of hooking up: announcing the hook up before it happens, as in saying, right before touching someone: Now we are going to touch.

But I must tell you, she says. We can't. We just can't.

Okay. Jed is relieved. For him, anything else might have ruined the day. Who knows? No problem, he says this a little too quickly, pretending earnestness. No problem at all.

I want to, she says, but we cannot be in a romantic relationship.

You don't have to explain, he says.

But Maggie explains. I have a boyfriend back in the States. He's a political scientist. An assistant professor.

Look at Jed now. He is inadequate. He's getting smaller. On the one hand, he wonders whether Maggie is lying about having a boy-friend—using him as a convenient excuse to end the date. Maybe he has said something offensive to her. Maybe she has some physical abnormality of which she is ashamed, a defect which would be exposed when naked. Maybe she is ashamed to admit that sex is, for her, unappealing. Or, that she prefers the emotional, rather than the physical, attention of another. Maybe, she prefers the romantic buildup to sex, the verbal games of suggestion and anticipation and the erotic delay, more than copulation itself. Or maybe, he thinks, she wants him to fight for her, to win her over despite the "boyfriend." On the other hand, he feels relieved and relaxed. The pressure is off. Now he breathes and leans back.

They sit for a long time looking out at the water. The waves lap against the nearby dock— they chase each other down.

That night, just before Jed goes to bed, Maggie texts him:

I have good news. I talked to my boyfriend. I told him that I met you and that we have developed a relationship. He said he wants me to have sex with you. He said he wants net happiness. He wants all good things for everyone. It's great news. Liberation and honesty. He's such a great boyfriend. He wants us to be open and free. Let's meet tomorrow.

After changing his mind many times, writing in his journal, looking up some definitions of various human emotions on the internet, Jed texts her back an eggplant emoji and a smiley face.

The next morning, he masturbates, but without porn, to extend his stamina without overloading his brain with serotonin. He takes a shower, puts on his best shirt, and prepares to leave his apartment.

Just before he slips on his sandals, someone

knocks on the door. It must be the landlord or the cleaner.

He opens it without looking through the viewer. There, standing at the threshold, are two large men. He looks at them, his mouth slightly open in confusion. They are dressed inconspicuously in jeans and t-shirts. They are wearing sunglasses.

Both enter the apartment uninvited.

Jed stumbles.

Have you been sleeping with Maggie?

What? I just met her. No.

The two men speak interchangeably, in turn, as if reading a script. That's not what we heard, says one, and the other repeats it.

I swear to God, Jed says. Look at my phone if you want. Here it is. She told me she had a boyfriend, so we didn't have sex, and then she said to me that her boyfriend was cool with everything. He said we had his permission to have sex. But I haven't done anything.

But you thought about it. The men step forward. You wanted it.

Now Jed's back is against the wall. What? No. No, I haven't

Thinking is the same as doing, says one. Whosoever looketh on a woman to lust after her hath committed adultery with her already in his heart, says the other.

One man steps forward and punches Jed in the jaw, knocking him to the floor. The other man stomps on his stomach.

Jed cries out. He cries.

The first man throws another punch to the face, hitting Jed in the nose. The second man holds him down by the back, while the first man repeatedly kicks him in the head and ribs. Over and over. Already he is bruised and bleeding from the nose and mouth.

While they beat him, Jed thinks about Maggie. Specifically, he is thinking about having sex with her on her apartment balcony, overlooking the city and the sea. He has no control over his thoughts. He imagines her naked body, her dark hair. He can hear her screaming his name. He sees her shoulders and neck dripping with sweat. He can see her clearly, more clearly now than before. Her absence makes her somehow more real. The sun is getting hotter. The sun draws closer and intensifies and grows. The sun overtakes him—a flame white disc. Now the world disappears and all there is to see is light, and out of the light appears an enormous angel holding a great spear at the tip of which burns a small fire, and the angel plunges the spear several times into Jed's heart and stomach, and Jed moans in agony and ecstasy. When the angel finally pulls the spear away and departs, Jed feels utterly consumed by what he can only call the love of God—cold and hot, gentle and violent.

So palpable is Jed's fantasy that, even while the men continue to punch and kick him in the chest and face, he feels an internal orgasmic climax, an elemental discharge, spiritual satisfaction.

The men are pounding and pounding until

—when their work is done, when Jed is sufficiently beaten—they leave.

Look. Jed is alone on the floor. At first, he feels euphoria and transcendence. A spiritual glory. A holy pain so extreme that he wished for it to go on forever. Now what does he feel? Relief, maybe. Gratitude. And now what? Now, pain, loneliness, confusion, shame, discontentment with anything less than the unconditional love of God.

Jed calls his landlord, and his landlord calls an ambulance. It turns out, Jed has five cracked ribs, three broken teeth, a broken nose, and a fractured collarbone. Also, he has a severe concussion, and his eyesight is irreparably damaged. He stays in the hospital for several days and thinks, for the first time in a long time, that he is truly alive.

He never hears from Maggie again. He texts her once, twice—but no response.

When his condition is stable, Jed returns to the US, but because of his damaged eyes, he can no longer work as an editor. For the next few years, he will take on various odd jobs around the city: a grocer, a doorman, a professional dog walker.

Now he sits alone in his apartment, looking out of the window. The sun has not yet risen. The air smells like burnt milk and fried food. He's unsure how to occupy his free time. He thinks about what to think about and keeps coming back to the same thing. His religious experience. He realizes that he wants nothing more than to feel it again—to see, if only once more, the face of that terrifying angel.

Soon Jed sets out on a mission to replicate the out-of-body experience he had in Barcelona. He goes into bars and provokes fights. Regularly men much larger than him beat and brutalize him—a chipped tooth here and there, a few bruises, a cut lip, a black eye. But he never approximates transcendence. He feels only pain.

Eventually, he places advertisements on craigslist, offering cash for specific types of violence. He pays other men to punch him in the stomach, kick him in the chest, cut him a little, choke him, spit in his eyes, piss in his face.

More years pass. Jed's search for transcendence becomes unsustainable and detrimental to his long-term health. Some of his beatings get out of hand and send him to the hospital. He struggles to hold regular employment because he cannot physically work. His life spirals down and down. He cannot pay his rent or hospital bills. And he returns home to live with his mother.

Why exactly did those men beat him in Barcelona? Because of Maggie? Had they said anything about staying away from her? No, they hadn't. They simply asked him a question and then beat him. Who were they to Maggie, and Maggie to them? Did they even know her? Did she send them? Did her boyfriend send them? Wasn't Maggie's boyfriend an academic? A political scientist? Wasn't he a respectable assistant professor at Stanford University? Had Maggie invented her boyfriend? Had she planned to hurt Jed all along? Was it a game? Why hadn't she ever called or texted? Was she even studying literature at Brown University? Had she even read *2666*?

At the end of the novel, Jed lies alone in bed and wonders what had made that initial beating so euphoric. Was it the adventure he'd been looking for since he'd moved to New York City? Or was he just a pervert? Some self-loathing weirdo? Maybe it was none of that. Maybe it was just a manifestation of shock? A confused physiological response to trauma? A coping mechanism? See? Maybe there's no mystery at all.

PART FOUR

20

In the opening stanzas of *Inferno*, Dante describes what it felt like, for me, to wake from a seizure. Completely alone. Disoriented. *In the middle of this thing called life, I found myself lost in a dark forest. Savage, arduous, extreme. The way was blotted out. There was no sky.*

This is what it feels like, except worse. Worse because momentarily, after a seizure, you have no concept of yourself—you cannot say, *myself.* You cannot say *lost* because you do not know what it means. Cannot say *in a forest* because you have no concept of being somewhere that is not somewhere else. Thrown by a cruel god into nothing recognizable.

It was the day after the protest.

I woke up. Where was I?

Oh. I'd shat myself. I woke up, just like that. In my own piss and shit and dried blood. I had never had a seizure that bad. I'd never shat myself before. I'd never even wet the bed.

I smelled like milk rot and mucus.

Bruised jaw. Split tongue.

I sat up and looked around and waited for a few minutes, allowing my eyesight to adjust and my mind to cohere and, when it did, cleaned myself up and thought about Janice.

Janice wouldn't be ashamed of me, why should I be? I shouldn't. I should be proud. And for a moment I was. I was a new man, why not?

I reached for my phone, but it wasn't there. I looked in my backpack and under my pillow and inside my pants and shoes and realized that I had left it in the pocket of my overshirt, and my overshirt was in Zeke's bag. I opened my laptop and used it to text Janice. When I didn't get a response, I called her. She didn't answer. I called again.

The wind blew in waves against the window and the glass rattled periodically. A brownish light slanted and dust hung stubbornly in the air, drifting in conflicting angles so that all I saw was dust. I pulled the blanket over my head, and slept, and—for the first time in years—dreamed. In my dreams, I saw alternative versions of the protest. I saw everything that could have gone differently. Some versions were more violent. In one version, I saw myself attacked, ambushed, mugged from behind. In another version, I became the aggressor, throwing punches and smoke bombs. In one version, I was completely naked and couldn't find my clothes.

When I woke, I ate a vegan burrito that wasn't really vegan and made a cup of tea and stood by the window and pretended to smoke and felt ridiculous and awkward, so I started to smoke for real, inhaling and exhaling and letting the smoke go deep into my throat.

I was living twice.

The traffic outside my window was unusually busy; cars and trucks passed quickly, and the speed of all that traffic instilled a worry in me that it was somehow later in the day that I believed it was—that my clocks were wrong, that I was falling behind the time, that I had missed the news of some important event, and I was now doomed to experience its aftermath.

Once I settled back into myself and remembered everything that had happened the night before, I could think more clearly. Was Zeke Janice's partner? Why hadn't she introduced him as such? Was she keeping it a secret? What else was she hiding from me? And also: Had I done enough to say I belonged to Antifa? Had I earned my tote bag? Had I sufficiently turned my lie into my life?

From my laptop, I called Janice again. Nothing. I thought to call Zeke, but remembered he didn't have a phone.

I waited.

The internet was there. Images and headlines and memes. I saw videos of airplanes bombing villages in Iraq and Turkey. I saw videos of protesters in Iraq breaking into the US Embassy. Another drone killing civilians. Another bum fight. I read articles, too—not full articles, but headlines. I was bombarded with a relentless stream of outrageous headlines. How is it, I wondered, that we can go on living—working, studying, writing poems and novels after this and this and this? So much to protest, it was hard to keep up. I watched videos of the protests in D.C. over and over. In one video: burning trashcans. In another: screaming, crying, and indiscriminate gunshots. As I watched the footage, the pain and suffering of others flickered before me, on the screen, and I felt, somehow, that I was seeing versions of my memories, or visions of my future.

21

Three days passed and still no word from Janice and now I was getting anxious and needed to talk to someone. I called Parker on FaceTime but when he answered his voice sounded faraway like an echo traveling across a lake.

Can you sit closer to the screen? I can't hear you at all.

Dude, he said. Come to a party tonight.

I made a thinking sound. I was thinking of something else: Janice and what I was going to do next. I sucked air between my teeth and repeated the sound. I don't think I can make it, I said. I'm writing. I'm working on my novel. Things are finally starting to happen.

•

I didn't go to the party but went out looking for Janice. If she wasn't going to come to me, I'd go to her. Also, I needed my phone back.

I went where I expected her to be—the café, the overpriced Mexican restaurant, and the officially unofficial Marxist bar called The Proletariat, where I knew Janice liked to hang out—hoping to bump into her. I went to campus, too, but the entrances were shut down and populated with police. I went back to Writer's Block. I waited for her while I sat flipping through a book, looking at the pages without reading.

I decided, finally, to go to her apartment.

I went trekking down Telegraph, striding it out with conviction, jaunting, about to break into a sprint. I kept my head down, weaving—turning my shoulders to make myself narrow—between and through and past the crowd, bounding by sheer intuition so as narrowly to miss the other walkers, occasionally grazing an item of clothing, a shirt sleeve or the corner of an open jacket, but never making physical contact with anyone. The street was vibrant and busy and packed with people, but I went faster. A body sensing other bodies. I went faster, pushing myself to an uncomfortable level. Soon, fast became too fast and I couldn't maintain that level of fluidity, and I bumped into someone—a man. I ran into him. He stepped into my path. I knocked him backward a step.

The man was dressed in uniform, a police officer.

Had he been standing there already? Had he seen me from a distance and—displeased with the pace of my almost-running—decided to slow me down? Was I breaking the law? My mind conjured memories real and unreal, memories of the protest and the police.

I admit I hit the officer. I knocked him off balance; and he stumbled to such a degree that, if you saw it from the periphery, it must've looked as if I'd pushed him. Had I pushed him?

The sun was hot. It was not a good position I was in. A small crowd began to congregate around the officer and me—seemingly eager to see why I had done it, and how the officer would retaliate.

One bystander reached into his pocket, took out his phone and, as if anticipating conflict, held it up to eye-level to film. Another bystander, when he saw the first, took out his phone, too, and held it up.

The policeman stepped forward. He lunged a single stride in the semblance of my own striding, and looked down on me with his oversized sunglasses, the kind that cover the space between the eyes and the temple, the eyes and the cheekbones, the eyes and the forehead. No light gets through.

I could see myself reflected in the sunglasses, too, standing there beneath him, looking at myself but seeming to look at him, where the eyes would be.

Unthinkingly, I apologized to him; and when he did not respond, I apologized again and gave him my name, though he had not asked for it.

The dry afternoon air made my lips crack.

The officer still hadn't said a word, so I explained myself in a way that might account for his silence. I was on my way to work, I said. Second work, I said. I mean, second job. I was coming from my first job on campus. I'm a web designer, at the university, and I was headed south, I said now, to my second job. And I was running late and had to walk faster than usual. Faster than normal. You know, I said. It's not usually like this. Normally I walk like everyone else.

I saw myself in his glasses. I was talking fast, I knew that, and I worried that I was undermining my cause—that the form of my speech might subvert its message. So, I began to counterbalance my speech by speaking slowly.

I usually take my time, I said, slow. I listen to news podcasts. I'm a good person.

He remained expressionless, mouth flat, jaw pulsating. His face was blank and vacant—a reflective surface onto which I was called to project myself. His nostrils flared in and out.

The surrounding crowd seemed to be growing. People were saying things to each other. I heard them but couldn't process their words—their words were not words at all but jumbled, unintelligible mouth-noises. Hissing, grunting, exhalation turning into static, white noise, random electrical signals, fluctuating voltages.

Sense seemed to dissipate, and an imaginary weight pressed down on me. I put my finger to my lips and did not answer again to that blank visage.

Finally, the policeman spoke. He lifted his arm and pointed his finger in the direction I had been going. Run, he said.

Run?

Run.

I went on, turning and proceeding slowly, unsure whether to take his command seriously.

No, he said. Run.

I picked up the pace, speed walking now.

Run, he cried.

I ran.

Run!

I went faster and soon I couldn't feel my

legs, my chest. I ran past the chained-up bikes, the trashcans and the accompanying recycling bins, the "exotic gift" store, the Kathmandu imports, the coffee nook and the sock shop and the hat store, past the Berkeley autocrat, and the gas station, and the nondenominational Christian church, past the redwood forest mural, the ocean mural, the mural commemorating the settling of Berkeley, the mural of the arrival of immigrants in Berkeley after the great San Francisco earthquake of 1906, past Oregon and Russel and Ashby Ave. I had a mind to walk all the way to Oakland, and I almost did—walking south again, in the rhythm of sidewalk trees, Chinese Tallows and Ginkgo, so redundant they were almost impossible to see, thin and leafless. People walked past me. They looked at me. They smoked cigarettes with their headphones in. I was humiliated, ashamed to be seen. I felt myself resisting something. I thought about the policeman. I hated him and the fact that he, by saying nothing, seemed to expect my confession, and I resented that confession—vulnerability, honesty—had become such a dominant mode of culture, of the internet, of Instagram poetry, of therapy, of religion. Tell everyone everything. Explain yourself. Emotions and public events. Self-expression and spectacle. In my mind, I was making an argument for secrecy. And maybe, I thought, for Antifa. And suddenly I felt justified in participating in the protest the previous night, justified in my aggression toward the police. This excited me and made me feel, somehow, physically closer to Janice.

I had already long passed her apartment. All that mattered now was my freedom—to get as far away as possible. The moonlight was chalk. It blurred everything it touched.

22

The sunrise backlit the hills, causing them to appear two-dimensional, surface level and flat, like cardboard cutouts, and cast an array of pale lights into the sky, the color of pus. Someone was sawing down a tree near my window.

More and more days were spent looking and not looking for Janice, though I slowed down to avoid the police. I went to her apartment daily. She was nowhere.

I continued to do my work—writing, not writing—but my entire conception of time and space was dictated by searching for Janice. Time moved as in a plot, determined by a sequence of cause-and-effect events, points, false climaxes, dead ends. This happened each time I went looking for her—when I wasn't looking for her, I was thinking of new ways to find her, new strategies and places to look. Everything that wasn't an event was idle waiting. I brushed my teeth four, five times a day.

I had a bad intuition that Janice had been seriously hurt or arrested. That she had been taken by the police for disturbing the peace, breach of the peace, public intoxication, unruly public behavior, excessively loud noise, assault. I went down, down to the police station, the courthouse, the county detention center, the jail, the prison. I inquired whether a certain prisoner had been brought in, arrested, tried, or convicted. I didn't say that word, prisoner, of course, because of its archaic tone, its implication of guilt—I knew how to use my words—but used, in its place, the more official-sounding "detainee," and the neutral terms "citizen" and "person." Everywhere I was told the same no. No such person had not been arrested, they said.

I didn't believe them.

At home, I called again—down to the police station, the courthouse, the detention center, the jail, the prison. And I asked a second time. Has there been a certain citizen, civilian, person placed under arrest?

•

To change my state of mind, I decided to do something Janice would do: to cook a proper meal, something from scratch, something warm and whole and real. Power curry soup.

I rode my bike to the grocery store—the one that advertised itself as a health food market, stocked with overpriced health, unfiltered or hyper-filtered, a parody of eco-friendly marketing, plant sausage, sausage plants, bacon extract, lard lotion, rutabaga candy, zero-chocolate chocolate bar, spruce juice, raw milk—and bought what my phone told me what to buy. Lentils, kale, sweet potatoes, tomatoes, celery, carrots, curry, rice.

It pleased me to touch real food.

At home, I laid out the ingredients on my bed and saw that I had a problem. In a moment of shortsightedness, I'd forgotten that I would need to use the communal kitchen to cook. And not only that, but also there was the problem of kitchenware. I owned nothing—neither cutting knife nor board to cut on. I opened my bedroom door just enough to hear whether anyone was nearby, waited a minute and hurried into the kitchen, carrying everything I could. I dropped the carrots in the hallway and had to go back for them once I set the remaining ingredients on the counter. I followed the directions—pulled the kale leaves from the stem and diced them. I chopped the carrots. I moved quickly, eager to finish the job before anyone came into the kitchen. I was chopping faster than my hands could move, and almost cut myself—twice the knife grazed my skin without breaking it. And I saw in my mind: myself cut, being cut.

My eye moved and fixed on the finger—my finger, there. Flat on the cutting board, next to the carrot, holding the carrot in place.

And then it happened.

I cut the finger.

It happened so fast that, at first, I wasn't sure whether the cut was real, or whether it was merely part of that long sequence of chopping vegetables. But soon I knew. It was more than a cut, more than a blade piercing the skin. I knew it. I cut the tip of the finger completely off, away from the hand, as if the finger had been part of the carrot it held.

Blood jumped out and ran and ran across the kitchen counter. And my first fear was not for the finger itself, the loss of finger, but for the blood: I worried I would be caught bleeding in the kitchen, and that this would be my long-anticipated introduction to the household.

I grabbed a paper towel and wrapped it around my finger to stop the bleeding, but the blood soaked through.

Is the finger worth saving?

I examined the cut-off flesh, the smallest tip of my finger, now laying on the floor where it had fallen. It was too small to sew back on and too small to make any functional difference for me anyway. I wrapped my finger in another paper towel and, with my free hand, squeezed the finger as hard as I could, and grabbed a wad of dish rags and paper towels and began to scrub the blood on the counter. My scrubbing, however, only served to smear the blood around in large circular patterns. I wet the rags and wrung them out and scrubbed again and looked under the sink and found bottles of disinfectant and stain-remover and took the two bottles and doused the entire countertop with them. Quick and frantic. Wiping and wiping again. I was aware that at any moment someone might come and that I would have to explain to them who I was, where I had been, and why now—now, here—I was bleeding in the kitchen.

But my actions canceled themselves out. Even as I cleaned up the blood, my finger continued to bleed. As I wiped away blood here, my finger cast new blood there.

I placed all my food into the communal refrigerator. Then I grabbed the knife I had used to cut myself, marked with my blood, and ran into my room and closed the door and stood by the window, still clutching the knife in one hand and my cut finger in the other.

Slowly I unwrapped my finger to see whether the bleeding had stopped.

Not yet.

Dizzy now. Now dazed and a little fuzzy in the head. I stumbled. My vision blurred. I looked down at the knife and thought, ridiculously, that I could do more than cut my finger. I could, I thought, take that very same knife and finish myself. Why not? I had the knife in the proper place, a few inches from my neck, and from my heart. I pointed it toward me and drew the blade closer to myself. I shocked myself doing it—how close I got to the flesh. Nothing could be easier.

Where do these thoughts come from?

I looked down at my broken wristwatch.

I thought about my mother.

I thought about Janice.

What was I living for?

23

I went to my appointment with the therapist. I kept my finger wrapped in gauze and kept my hand in my pocket so that he couldn't see it.

The therapist didn't greet me in his usual way—didn't say hello, didn't ask how our week was, how our work was going, or what do we feel like talking about. Today he went to the point. Maybe he sensed that we were running out of time. That we hadn't made any progress in the five previous meetings.

How's our writing? he asked. Our novel?

We quit that novel, I said.

The novel about Simon? Why did we quit? Are we quitting writing forever?

We want to quit.

We want to, or we will?

We want to, but we can't.

Why can't we?

Because what else would we do?

We could do anything, we're still young.

We're not that young.

No, he agreed. We're not that young.

We'll keep writing.

Do we have a new idea?

We might.

Do we want to talk about it?

The story?

The story.

Fine.

Tell me.

I felt my finger throbbing in my pocket. I thought about the blood and knife, and I made up a new story. This was it:

Franz, I said, a middle-aged banker, wakes up one morning paralyzed with a sense of remorse and guilt. Maybe it's the feeling that he's wasted his life. He gets out of bed and makes lemon tea in a pot, pours it into a porcelain mug and adds milk. As he sips, his head becomes clearer, and he remembers what in sleep he was able to forget—the night before, in a fit of rage, he killed a man. He murdered Vernon, his childhood friend. A sense of horror takes him over. He's racked with guilt and regret. It's killing him, yes, those are his exact words. It's killing me. He repeats them like a prayer. I'm already dead. Franz decides to confess to the murder and liberate his soul. That's what he says. To release my soul, whatever that is. As he's walking to the police station to confess, Franz plays and replays, in specific detail, the method by which he killed the man, how he beat him to a pulp, stabbed him three times in the abdomen, cut his hair off, clipped his fingernails, and put him in the bathtub to bleed. He rehearses the killing in his mind over and over so that, when called upon, he can accurately represent the event in language. When Franz gets to the police station, he confesses without hesitation. He repeats again in painstaking detail how he killed his friend. He even notes the exact direction the blood went when it hit the ground, and how it indicated to him a slight tilt in the floor. But the police don't believe him. In turns out, they have no report of any such murder. And not only that. They can't even find a record of anyone named Vernon Rodgers in the entire city. No such person even exists. They check to see whether Franz's confession matches any other recent murders in the area, but no. Nothing. Franz remembers committing a crime that never happened. He proceeds to wander the city aimlessly, enumerating the details of his crime repeatedly. Everything is vivid and real; his sorrow is undeniable. He cries for his lost friend, sure, but he cries harder—he weeps—for the inability to atone for his sins. For hundreds of pages, he talks to himself about the nature of his guilt. Is it personal, social, political, spiritual? He does everything he can think of, but there is no escape from it. He confesses to a priest. He sees a therapist. But no. No single institution can assuage his pain. No confession either. He wonders whether it was all a bad dream. He calls Vernon, but Vernon's number is disconnected. He searches for Vernon's email, but there is no such email in his inbox or list of contacts. Eventually, Franz concludes that Vernon never existed, that the murder was a dream, a vision. But for how long had he imagined Vernon to be real? Franz goes on trying to interpret his dream, but he cannot. There is no fully adequate interpretation. All interpretations bear some merit. There are good interpretations and bad interpretations. Correct ones and incorrect ones. For example: Is Vernon the embodiment of a lost future? An alternative life? Franz tries to induce dreaming—to have the same dream again.

Night after night, he takes drugs. He drinks heavily, mixing liquor with red wine. He watches horror movies right before falling asleep, turns up the heat, wears socks to bed, swallows pain pills, estrogen pills, Chinese fertility pills—everything the internet recommends. Nothing works. He has all the wrong dreams, all the wrong nightmares. Soon, he comes to the inevitable conclusion that Vernon is a version of himself. But which version? Why should he be murdered? Why should Franz be the one to murder him?

How does it end? asked the therapist in a voice suddenly deep.

I pressed my cut finger into my palm. You can probably guess how it ends, I said. Franz kills himself in the exact manner that he dreamed of killing Vernon. Three times in the chest. Haircut. Fingernails. Bathtub. The whole scene.

The therapist paused and looked at his watch and ran his fingers through his hair. So, he said, shuffling loose sheets of different colored paper around on his lap in such a way that made his question seem offhanded. So, he said again. In this version of the story, are we Vernon or Franz?

24

It happened like I thought it would. As soon as I stopped looking for Janice, she found me.

It was Thursday. I didn't notice the rain until it had stopped raining. It looked like it might rain again, but I went out and rode my bike anyway. Light reflected off the scattered pools of rainwater like parts of a broken tool.

There was a book sale at Writer's Block, and the store was unusually crowded and muggy. Poets, people who looked like poets in leather jackets. Students in flannel shirts and white linen pants and white socks and see-through tops and low-cut V-necks. More people poured in. The front door slammed shut again and again and the little bell tied to the handle banged repeatedly against the door like the chirp of a smoke detector.

Then I felt someone's fingers pressing down on the back of my neck. I stood up and shook her hand businesslike. I thought you'd been arrested, I said, almost whispering, so as not to be overheard.

Janice pressed her mouth close to my ear. Arrested?

Or hurt, I said. I don't know.

She smiled and lifted my phone out of her pocket and slapped me in the chest with it and waved it in front of my face. No way, she said. They didn't get me. Not yet.

She handed me the phone. *The social up-*

heaval of the 60s meets the political polarization and institutional dysfunction of the present. Forty-eight percent of the country believes a civil war is coming.

It turned out, disappearing was what Janice tended to do, and she knew how to do it. She explained that, after a run-in with the police—after any form of public unrest in which she may become implicated—she'd leave town. Men do it all the time, she said. Why can't I?

When I asked her where she'd gone, she responded: High and dry. To hide for a while. Recharge.

Okay.

Okay.

Okay.

Holy fuck, she said.

What?

Janice reached out and grabbed my finger and pulled it up to her face.

I let out a little whimper.

What happened to your finger? Someone cut you?

No.

No?

It was an accident.

Good Christ.

Forget it. Want to do something? Should we get lunch, or what?

She thought. She looked around. Let's go hiking, she said. Let's go up to the mountains.

Right now?

•

Next thing was, we were hiking. Took my car and drove east of town, west of the San Pablo Reservoir. We walked a narrow hiking trail, thinning down to a ghost trail—barely one—that meandered and rose along the ridge and down again into the ravine.

Weeds and tall grass grew across the way we went. The thunder clapped and the sky darkened, and a light swept across the surface of the reservoir.

Janice moved fast, and I struggled to keep pace. I stopped to breathe and wiped sweat from my forehead and placed my hands on my knees and bent my elbows and leaned onto them. She was talking about something; I couldn't hear what. She ran ahead and then stopped and turned around and shouted: Let's go. Come on!

Now came the rain, slowly at first and then faster: very soon the trail was muddy, and I had to exert more effort than I wanted to lift my foot with each step, so that walking was labored and awkward. I heard a sound that resembled laughter, was someone laughing at me?

This rain, I said. Maybe we should turn around?

Janice ignored me. She pushed on, against what felt like a growing wind.

Sorry, I said, louder now. Maybe we should head back!

Janice tamped down the mud as she went, and I fit my feet into her footprints, though I had to extend my stride to keep up with her, and for several minutes I walked with myself. The wind was louder and faster. I lost Janice's voice inside the noise of it, gargled and faint now. And as the wind quickened, Janice did too. She lengthened her stride so that now it was too long for me to follow, and I had to trudge across the untouched mud on my own.

The trail turned from the vista and dropped down and around, across a field of boulders. It went further down, and I could not see in front of me. We were moving downhill. It felt that way. Down a ledge and past a cluster of burned land, charred and brittle trees and grass and brush. I called out to her. I slipped on an errant root and fell, face down toward the trail, and extended my arm to brace myself and cut the palm of my hand on a rock which was hidden beneath fallen leaves. Hey, I cried out. Hey! I stood up and wiped my bloody palm against my jeans, and it hurt. It was swollen and enlarged and dirty. I cried out again, and a voice in the distance cried out in response. Jesus! said the voice, which I now recognized as Janice's. Jesus!

I went down, and father down, and followed the trail another twenty yards through a dry meadow and down to the edge of the reservoir. I couldn't say how Janice got so far ahead of me.

She stood over what I immediately identified to be a carcass, though couldn't tell right away what the thing was or had been.

Come look.

I couldn't look.

Come on, she said. This is insane. She pointed down. Look.

I looked and saw the carcass of that unidentifiable animal, which had been, she said, a goat, though it had no distinguishing shape. The torso had been split open, disfigured and mutilated and contorted unnaturally, as if having been pulled in two opposing directions. Flesh hung there. Maggots. Flies. Worms. The skull was detached from the spine and broken along the crown, and its intestines and viscera spilled onto the dirt the color of the dirt itself. As I looked, the entrails and innards seemed to move closer to my eyes, so close that I could not see it, or see past it. Everything amassed together into a single wreck of unholy gum, viscous and waxy. I understood that what I saw there was the mechanisms of existence, the raw thingliness, the constituents and meaty stuff of life without the thing called living. The closest thing to *real*, maybe. Or the furthest.

It's a good omen, Janice said. Very good.

I'm sick.

Janice smiled. It looks like Pad Thai, yum.

She was right, kind of. It was then that I began to experience a sudden ingestion and digestion, as if I had been eating the thing I looked at.

Now I was heaving.

It is universal law, I was reading in some magazine, she said, that one thing should resemble another, and that the chain of resemblance should lead back to some original thing.

More heaving.

Well, she said, still pointing. Here it is.

I stumbled away and vomited just off the trail, angling my mouth away from my body so that I wouldn't spit up anything onto my pants. I had to sit down. A voice said my name. Voices. Buzzing. Ringing. Great War drums beating in the distance.

Janice was laughing like a god.

25

After that, weeks passed in frenzy and love, in righteous anger, in mania and compulsion. What happened on Monday happened on Wednesday and Friday, a different action in the same place. I attended all the rallies, whatever their cause. I went with Janice and sometimes Julio came, too. I wore my own black clothes and cried out and chanted and held my own homemade sign and marched with the masses and danced with them and sang their songs. It felt right to be there—to feel myself lost among something relevant and communal, to hear my voice blend and fade into a collective prayer—to let it blend. I carried my tote bag proudly: three arrows pointing down.

And I went to Antifa gatherings. I assumed they were meetings, officially or unofficially, but Janice called them *parties*. She introduced me to some of the others. A tall man with a burned chin. A horse's face. A short guy with green and silver hair. A man dressed up like a baby. A college student in leather pants. A mohawk. A mullet. Nice to meet you. Welcome. Welcome. Nice to meet you. I met Eliot, who studied film at Harvard, and Ryan, who studied theater at UC Santa Cruz, and Lisa who studied philosophy at Stanford, and Kenneth, who went to Yale, and Hannah and Terry and Gloria and Lawrence, who all studied Comparative Literature at UCLA, and Marilyn and Roy and Alan and Beverly and Sophia and

James, who had attended the Iowa Writers' Workshop. (Janice introduced me as a writer, but none of the other writers seemed to care.) All of them had something to say, and they said it with the same voice. They spoke the language of revolution. I was a *comrade*. The police were fuzz, pigs, bacon, fat hogs. The enemy was the facho or fash. They talked about their guns. They said, if the government gets to have them, we get to have them, too. We don't rely on the cops or courts. Guns and grenades. They talked about their love and their hatred. One said, I hate this goddamned country and that's what makes me a patriot. Another said, only when you hate America are you truly American. They told stories of violence and victory. They told me about fires and pipe bombs and tear gas and pepper spray. They enumerated their run-ins with the fuzz, the bacon. Unlawful entry at a protest at a school. Unlawful assembly during the National Convention. Unlawful possession. Unlawful carry. Unlawful transportation of machine gun, military firearm, sawed-off shotgun. Assaulting a police officer at a World Bank protest. Assaulting a police officer at an IMF protest. Punching a Nazi. Kicking a Nazi in his mouth, neck. We are prepared to put our bodies on the line. Me too. Me too. I listened. I was happy to listen. I believed everything. I wanted everything. I inserted myself into their stories and saw myself there, among the indignant, the militia of justice and progress. I wanted to hear, to listen, and to try to understand. I felt I was at the center of the world. I felt a mixture of dread and excitement. A youthful fantasy. A lizard thrill. Adrenal toxins flowing through the bloodstream. A series of flashing and visions and images and abstracted bodies. The sexual self seeing itself as in a dream. A sex dream. The scent of bodies lingering and laying together—vinegar and onions. Then another wave. Intoxication. Breathing fast. Then a gaping hole opening in the floor.

All this newfound confidence was productive. Sleep came easily. Wakefulness, too. I ate healthy foods like kombucha and kimchi and kale chips. I ate five or six meals a day, trying to satisfy some hunger, a hunger for nothing and everything at once. A hunger for experience and the experience of experience. A hunger to live again. I worked and watched the internet. I rode my bike to see and be seen. I did what people do. There was always that noise, noise within noise—construction and conversation, breaking down and building.

In the news: police brutality and violent uprisings. Fires in the Santa Cruz mountains. Earthquakes in Los Angeles. Riots in Sacramento. Government surveillance. Wars and rumors of wars. In town, excitement and rage and sex and signs and flags and picks. The people were everywhere, out in the light, men and women and children in the streets and the quads and the public spaces, campaigning and marching and picketing, threatening to shut down any dissenting voice. We agreed with each other. We seemed to agree. We touched hands and took pictures. Cars honked. Drum circles formed on campus and downtown,

on the steps of city hall and the public librar-
ies. The whole town vibrated with intensity and
movement, and I saw myself at the center of it.

I hummed around the town with my head
up, believing myself to be, at last, myself. The person I was supposed to be. I sat in public places, on
park benches and on the patios of cafes and bars.
I ate expensive pastries, sandwiches and cakes. I
wanted to be seen and noticed. I walked around
and around, in crowds of people at the grocery
store and the park and, though I didn't know
anyone, I felt that I recognized everyone. I waved
to them, the burly men and the athletic women,
the hippie-looking teenagers and the leather-skin
rock climbers and mountain bikers and rancher-
lookalikes. I clicked my teeth and whistled. Everything had its soul. Everything its spirit. I was
living twice. I had my cigarettes. But then, when
alone, I had daydreams of being with Janice—stupid hallucinations of running away with her, living in a little house somewhere else, cooking and
cleaning and waking up together.

26

I met Parker at McDonald's. We sat in the usual booth, but on opposite sides. I faced the door, and Parker faced the cash registers and kiosks. He wore a neon green jacket, the kind that swooshes every time you move inside it.

I looked around for Josh, my shepherd. Alas.

Are those new glasses? I said, though I knew they weren't.

No.

I felt a quiet hostility between us and didn't know whether it came from me or him.

What happened to your finger?

Cut myself.

Doing what?

Cooking.

What are you, eight years old.

The fluorescent lights pointed down as on a stage. The man behind Parker was gnashing his teeth, mashing over and over shreds of food that already looked fully digested. He smacked his lips and his tongue flittered, and he licked his lips, and licked past his lips, down to his chin, and smacked again. Chomped and clicked his tongue, teeth, and jaw. He was murmuring words under his breath, too, uttering a prayer. He looked out the window, watching, as if there was something to see. I watched him watching long enough that I also looked out—but there was nothing, nothing I could see. Just an ordinary street and its sidewalk, an intersection, stoplights, students with leather satchels, the unhoused.

Parker asked me why I hadn't gone to the party. I explained to him that I hadn't been feeling well.

A pause. A menacing silence.

I leaned across the table and placed my elbows on the surface of it. I saw myself: I was wearing black—a Nike hoodie. One that I'd owned for years, but rarely wore.

Parker reached underneath the table and took up his backpack, and, from his backpack, removed his book. Some novel. He threw it open and dropped his head. Maybe we should just read today, he said.

I slurped coffee, sucking the cup without lifting it off the table—it was hot, and I cooled it sloshing it between my lips before swallowing.

Parker looked up. I'm surprised you still drink coffee, he said. Didn't you see the New York Times article about coffee?

The one about hot drinks and stomach cancer?

He nodded.

You're eating fake meat, I said. You don't think that gives you cancer?

He leaned back and extended his arms to push his Big Mac wrapper away from his body. Everything gives you cancer, he said. Even the stuff that prevents cancer gives you cancer. You might have cancer right now and you don't even know it. I might get cancer in two weeks. You could smoke cigarettes your whole life, drink a bottle of wine every goddamned day, eat at McDonald's and never get cancer. Or maybe you eat healthy your whole life, and you get cancer at age thirty-five just because. Maybe you never wear sunscreen, and the sun gives cancer. Maybe you wear sunscreen and the chemicals in the sunscreen give you cancer. Maybe you get cancer because you drink too much alcohol and maybe you get cancer because you stop drinking alcohol. It's completely arbitrary.

Okay, so we're both going to die of cancer, like everyone else.

My point isn't about the cancer, Parker said. My point is about you. I can't believe *you* still drink it. You, who is afraid of everything.

Not anymore, I said.

He made a look.

I joined Antifa, I said. I marched with them at the protest the other day.

Antifa.

Yeah.

Antifa isn't a real thing. You know that, right?

Immediately I wondered whether this was one of those "Fight Club" type of situations. Parker is denying the existence of Antifa, I thought, because he *belongs* to Antifa, because he's upholding some code of conduct. He's testing me, I thought. Maybe he thinks me unworthy. Of course, Antifa is a real thing, but its members must deny it. A secret organization can only remain legitimate if it maintains its secret, right?

Suddenly I imagined all the potential secrets

that Parker wasn't telling me about Antifa: plots to undermine the police, overthrow the nation-state. A montage of images I had seen on the internet.

Sure, I said.

He looked at me like I'd just pissed on his shoe. Antifa is not an organization. There are no leaders, no membership, no meetings. A righ-twing boogeyman is what it is.

Parker didn't know what he was talking about. Or maybe he did.

Either way, later that night, something terrible happened. And it happened, I think, because Antifa was or was not real.

It happened with Zeke.

27

Janice called me and asked whether I wanted to have drinks with Zeke and I almost said no but didn't want Janice to think me jealous or unsupportive of her polyamory.

From Zeke's we can hit The Proletariat or whatever, she said.

This would prove to be a milestone in our relationship, I thought. I was invited, finally, to hang out with one of Janice's other lovers and for that I was—or felt I should be—grateful.

•

We took an Uber to Zeke's butcher shop. From there, we would walk over to his apartment through the park. Janice wore a weird buffalo plaid dress-thing that cut off at the knees—wool, thick, double-breasted, vague animal costume, and beneath it: black stockings that covered up her legs.

First thing, Zeke opened the door, and pointed at me. What's wrong with your finger?

I looked down.

You get cut?

I cut myself.

Why'd you do it?

It was an accident.

Doesn't look like an accident. You practically cut off your whole finger.

He was dressed in jean shorts and a flannel shirt with a similar black and red tartan pattern to Janice's bathrobe-thing, which he left unbuttoned to show his usual black t-shirt beneath. He wore stainless-steel butcher gloves that clicked when he used his hands.

He started closing shop, wiping down the counters and putting away everything small enough to fit inside a drawer. Then he asked me whether I wanted to see the meats.

The meats?

He took me in the back where he showed me what he cut and how he cut it: huge slabs of flesh that hung from hooks like dark raincoats in the walk-in freezer. He pointed to the right and to the left. Pigs, he said. Cows. Zeke prodded them. He said this is good and put his palm flat on a heaping block of meat and it swayed and rocked—red and white. He wiped his mouth with the back of his sleeve, and he pushed his hair back and scratched his nose. He hiccuped. He tightened the muscles on his neck and flexed his jaw. Then he leaned in, toward me, as if waiting to hear what I had to say.

I cleared my throat.

He pointed again. This is the round, he said. And there is the oyster steak. This is called the Aitch bone, and here the tendons. He pointed and jabbed. Here is the shank, and more tendons and ligaments. A tough bundle of muscles, he said. Good for braising. I'll unbundle the top round and seam the muscles apart tomorrow. He ran his finger down the carcass. Here the femur bone. Great winter meal, he grinned. Good marrow there. And here the knuckle. He pointed. Here the sirloin tip. Here's the eye round, the heel, and the knee. And there is the bottom round for roast beef.

I didn't recognize these clumsy shapes as animals at all.

He pointed. Say it, he said.

Say what?

That, he said. Aitch bone.

Aitch bone, I said.

He pointed. Shank.

Shank.

Say it.

Shank, I said.

Shank, he said. That's right.

I pointed. What about that?

That? That's just the connective tissue. Some blood, there. There. I'll cut it out later, for presentation. It's all about presentation, my work. Making the carcass look like an ordinary grocery item. And look at the pigs, he said. Over here. He pointed and stepped and looked back. Look here. He put his hand flat against it. The leaf lard. No taste in it, he said. I'll cut it. Cut it right off. Here the flank section. The sirloin. The tenderloin. The kidney. For sausage, he said. He knocked the swollen mass. The shoulder. The rib, there. The elongated muscles, see. There. More flank. The skin is dry, you see. The ham and the joints. The belly, there. Here. The whole thing.

•

When we got to Zeke's apartment, he told us to

shut up and have a seat and stomped into the kitchen and removed three small glasses—foggy, smudged with fingerprints—from the cupboard and set them on the coffee table in front of us and poured a splash of something green and hot into each.

Grass, he said.

Grass?

Tea, yeah. Grass tea. He stomped around, arranging things, tidying up. He wore Dr. Martens combat boots.

Janice lifted the glass to her nose and sniffed the drink, and she pulled back her hand, dropped her chin and scrunched her face and silently screamed. Gross, she said.

It's just grass.

It's literal grass.

Sorry, it's all I have. He sat down on the floor, spread his legs out so that I could see the outline of his crotch—the shape of a fist.

He gulped.

I could tell that Zeke was excited. His manners were bad. He got brash, showing off. He didn't know how to do polite talk, so he ranted about this and that, and he waved his hands around like a European. He sounded like a European, too, speaking with a certain exigency, a somber morality about the state of things: theories of being, theories of the universe, heaps of second-hand knowledge and useless information.

Janice looked at him sideways. What's wrong with you tonight?

He slapped himself in the face and smiled.

I'm hyped up, he said. I need to get out.

Janice, with a little smirk on her face, told him to show me his paintings.

You're a painter? I asked.

I used to be, he said.

Show me.

He stood up erect and reached beneath his bed and produced an elongated canvas—a painting. This is the only one I still have.

The painting was—I don't know what. It was a garden, maybe, but too messy to be a garden. A patch of earth. A thicket of tangled lines. Verdant, ornate. An overgrowth of interweaving vines, branches, bramble, grasses and weeds—in shades of green and brown, clumped and combed in layers. The perspective was unnatural. Too close or too far to see what it meant to show—too focused, not focused enough, too intimate, too detached. It looked more like the detail of a painting than a painting itself. It seemed to hide something rather than show it. And the brushstrokes were crude and sweeping so that each shape—each leaf and fond and petal, every limb and stalk and needle—only consisted of a single stroke, so that it all blended together.

The painting surprised me. On one hand, I thought it spiritual and sad—beautiful maybe, or not quite beautiful. On the other hand, it wasn't beautiful at all. It was the opposite of beautiful. And the longer I looked the less I knew what I was looking at. The technique was sloppy and careless, obscene even. And it felt as if I had walked in on someone taking a shit.

After looking at it for a long time—confused and nauseous—I said something general but praiseful. Interesting. Great technique.

Zeke put the canvas back where he got it. He lifted his mug and drank the grass tea entirely and set the mug down in the exact ring of moisture it had vacated.

Why'd you quit painting?

It's a long story, he said.

Tell him, said Janice.

Tell me.

Zeke told his story, and it went like this: When I'm young, they tell me that I can be whatever I want. They tell me, express yourself. And I do. I did. I study art. I bocame a painter. I'm trying to have my vision. After grad school, art school, I moved to Los Angeles. Lots of artists are moving there. I'm nostalgic for California. I have an idea of it and what it means. And I have a plan. You know how it goes, one takes a shitty job and works up into a given profession. I paint on the side. Neh. I get a studio apartment with the money I'd saved working at a grocery store in college. I eat the same thing every day, he said. Instant oatmeal in the morning, two bananas and peanut butter for lunch, and four packets of ramen noodles with three cans of tuna for dinner. I do five hundred pushups and seventy-five pull ups every morning. Without question. I spend a few hours looking for a job. And in the afternoon, I paint. I painted. I am never a more productive painter. Two months later, I've run out of money. I eventually take a job as a meat handler at a local grocery store. My commute is long, over an hour, extending my workday by two hours. Sometimes more. I don't have time to make friends. I don't have time to paint. I don't have time even to live. I'm not living at all. I hate my job. I'm restless, always looking for something else. Something better. When I'm not working, I'm looking for more work, better work. Twenty-four-seven. No sleep. Neh. So, I quit the job and I'm out of money, losing my mind. What else can I do? What should I have done? I have no choice. I am so unhappy I couldn't stand it. Aren't I supposed to be happy? But I can't get another job, man. Nothing. Losing money. I am possessed by an impulse to break things. To ruin everything. To destroy objects and break rules. At first, it was small things. I go into corporate elevators to fart. That kind of thing. Nasty. I scream at strangers in the street. I piss in public spaces—parking lots and restaurant patios. But it gets worse. Neh. I pretend to rob grocery stores, gas stations, banks. I start to masturbate in churches, right there, during the Sunday service. Right there. In the middle of the sermon. The preacher would be saying something about Jesus and the resurrection and I'm beating off in the congregation.

Did anyone notice you?

Zeke went on without answering the question. I'm losing my identity. And I start having recurring dreams. Dreams on a loop, night after night, dreams of trash. Landscapes of litter and waste. Mountains and oceans of debris and detritus. Plastic bottles, boxes, and wrappers. Tuna cans and beer kegs. Amazon packaging, grocery bags, plastic straws.

Did anyone notice you? Did anyone see you in the churches?

He went on. So, one day, my landlord comes in and tells me that he's kicking me out, he said. No explanation. Get out, he says. Neh. And I'm hysterical. I'm wandering the streets at midnight. No sleep. So, I up my workout regimen. More pull-ups and pushups. No rest. A sense of failure grows inside of me. No friends, no job, no place to live.

Zeke paused and inhaled and exhaled and pulled a cigarette out of his pocket. He slipped the cigarette into his mouth and held it loosely between his lips.

For a long time, I'm possessed. I'm not in control of my own actions, haunted by rage and violence. All-encompassing hatred. So, it comes to me: a plan. I'm going to hurt that fucker. I'm going to fuck up that landlord's whole life. This is the plan. Neh. My landlord lives four blocks away. So, I bike over three days in a row. Just to check on his house, see what's going on and all that. I find out that he has a dog, a Great Pyrenees. Massive white thing. The dog is mostly okay. He doesn't bark, mostly. Good dog. And he's outside in the back yard most of the day, when the landlord is away. Neh. I execute the plan to perfection. I ride my bike down the road to his house. I have all my keys in my pocket—two apartment keys, the key to the mailbox. That's three keys, man. That's perfect. The number of perfection. As I pull up, I take out my keys, place them in the palm of my hand and make a fist around them so one key protrudes out between two fingers. Like this. You see. A fist with three keys sticking out. One key for every finger hole. You know what I do. I walk right up to that dog. He's barking crazy, losing his mind. I start punching him in the face. Hard as I can. And the dog is squealing and crying so badly you'd think he was a human crying like a little boy. I keep punching him over and over, hitting him in the eye and the mouth. Neh. He's bleeding everywhere. Cuts all over his face, and he can't see. And he can't fight back because he's blind now. His face is pulp.

As Zeke spoke, I had the distinct feeling that it was raining, but when I looked at the window, it was not.

Zeke took out a lighter, and lit his cigarette, and puffed and exhaled into my face. A blue layer of smoke grew.

He went on. That was the night that I pack up and left. Heading north. Nowhere. Nothing but my shitty car and the clothes on my body. I drive up Highway One. I sleep by the side of the road. I scavenge for food in dumpsters outside of restaurants and bakeries in Santa Barbara, San Luis Obispo, Big Sur, Carmel, Monterey, Santa Cruz. Neh. I stay in Santa Cruz for a few months—pitched a tent near the highway with the rest of the drifters. We are all scavenging. The community of tents grows bigger and bigger by the week. During that time I see horrible things. I see grown men sexually molested, see them stabbed with shards of plastic and glass. And I see good things, too. Homeless folks pulling people out of burning cars, and sharing food, and carrying signs to protest the government. But here's the thing. This is the point. Neh. I am not unhappy there. I am not exactly happy either, but that's because happiness is a lie. I know that now. But I was fulfilled. Fulfilled because my life was finally my own.

I had wanted to stop Zeke and ask questions, but his story did not lend itself to interruption; and he seemed not to care whether I was listening. The purpose of his story, it seemed, was cathartic, rather than informative. My suspicion was confirmed when, at this point in the story, he started talking faster as if approaching a climax. An exhausted half-orgasm.

And I realize, he said, that the source of my shame. Frustration wasn't inside of me. It's out there, in the culture of machines and men—in cheap architecture and environmental collapse and addictive politics. It's a goofy thing about depression. Everyone says depression is a chemical imbalance in our brains, in our whole bodies. Something is wrong with us, they say. They use words like disorder, disease, sickness. They give us pills that make us complacent or passive. Neh. But they've got it wrong. We're not sick. Neh. The world is sick.

I looked at my broken wristwatch.

Then came the election, four years ago, the police riots started. The folks are angry. Marching and rioting in public. The folks are protesting government policy. The folks are protesting police brutality and democracy itself. And I feel drawn to this kind of life. Activism and instability. My life had purpose then, free from the sterile, optimistic mainstream.

I tugged at my cut finger.

My rage used to be undirected and unproductive. I was misguided. But now I know where to aim it. I have the gift of rage. The power and mysticism of negativity. Do you understand what I'm telling you, he said. Neh. Wrath is wiser than instruction.

But what about the dog? I asked. And the churches, did anyone see you in the churches?

•

A cover band played Joy Division at The Proletariat.

As soon as we walked in, some at the bar lifted their heads to watch us and nodded or didn't nod. Someone said Zeke's name. Someone shook his hand, and I noticed he was still wearing his work gloves. He introduced us to Billy and Roman and Angie and Nathan and Calvin and Paul. We went on and sat in a back booth—the cushions were small and firm and unusually close to the table. Zeke sat facing the entrance. Never face away from the entrance, he said. I sat across from him, next to the wall, and Janice slid in next to me.

A pendant light fixture swung low over the table.

I looked over my shoulder and saw two men looking back at me. I looked away and back and away again. I recognized one of them right away. I thought I did. It was the kid from the protest on campus. The boy. Tall and hairless, head shaved, dark eyes. It was him. And now he was with another guy (another boy, I thought), short and bearded.

Now I felt a sense of dread in my spine, my gut. I looked back to make sure I had seen what I saw. There they were—the same look as before, looking back.

I think I know those guys, I said.

Zeke nodded. I see them. I saw them when we walked in.

The waiter came by and called us comrades.

We ordered beers, and, trying to ignore the man-boys, we let our conversation turn to more mundane topics. We talked about whether we enjoyed living in the Bay Area. Janice said yes, but, she added, it's all become a little sterile. You know, losing its character. Like a giant strip mall. Everything looks the same.

Zeke agreed. He was severe and jagged where the light cast a shadow over the lower half of his face. He said yes, he mostly liked living here. Berkeley and San Francisco have always been on the cutting edge of politics, he said. But there are so many, how should I say it, milksops, panty-waists, posies. All of them with their heads down. And their world fits onto small screens. And they think small. Small as children. The men are castigated and impotent, and the women stressed out and neurotic.

I started to look over my shoulder, but Zeke

stopped me. Don't look. They're still there. I got eyes on them.

We ordered another round.

Beads of precipitation ran slantwise down the glass of beer in front of me, collecting at the base in a pool of moisture.

•

We stayed for another few hours at the bar, and when the man-boys finally left, we left, too. We meandered across the street to a bookstore, and then walked to other bars, The White Horse and The Dirty Bird and The Do-Over. Around three in the morning, everything was closed.

I think I'm done, I said.

Yeah, said Janice. I quit, too.

Zeke spoke in his deepest voice. Let's walk it off.

And we did walk. Zeke lifted his finger and pointed forward and we followed. Janice walked in long strides, lunging, the way one walks downhill, not so much walking as preventing oneself from falling.

Zeke went ahead of us, humming something low and guttural. His stride was long, a soldier's stride—mechanical and automatic, he brought his knees up to his waist, almost marching.

I felt like I was inside Zeke's painting: figures and objects flattened against black and grey swirls of painted wind, still wet, slowly spinning, circles within circles, thicker and thinner intermittently, and textured with eggshell and sand, twirling in directional strokes, pressing counter-clockwise against us as we walked. The houses leaned forward into the streets, and the streets were coated in blue shadows that fell from the objects they failed to copy.

The phone vibrated. *A shadowy science institute, funded by food and drug industry giants, has been quietly infiltrating government agencies around the world. A 10-year-old Texas girl who contracted a brain-eating amoeba swimming in a lake and river near Waco has died. A new group of extremists who are venturing out of chat rooms and into the real world with firearms defy easy categorization.*

Where were we now?

The streetlights were becoming less frequent, and there were only occasional patches of light into which the surrounding cityscape appeared and disappeared, like a puzzle with missing pieces.

Zeke was still wearing his stainless-steel butcher gloves—he hadn't taken them off, not once, and he clapped them together as he sang: I saw ten thousand talkers whose tongues were all broken, I saw guns and sharp swords in the hands of young children.

We moved with our heads down, following the sound of Zeke's voice. Janice occasionally leaned over and bumped into me, a little harder each time—once almost knocking me completely off balance. She was flirting, I think, reminding me that she was still there. Or else she was genuinely stumbling, struggling to stay upright.

Zeke went on and on singing about the

apocalypse, and I wondered whether he really wanted the world to end—to abolish borders and burn cities—or whether he presented the most extreme possible versions of his politics to hyperbolize his commitment. He sang louder and louder, as if to announce himself to the surrounding darkness: *I heard thunder, it roared out a warning. Heard the roar of a wave that could drown the whole world.*

A long time passed and suddenly, for reasons I can't explain, I felt apprehension or dread. And I would struggle, in the days to come, to sort out the following events.

Here's what happened.

I heard someone walking close to us, closer, coming from behind. The distance between us seemed to collapse and I turned to see what was there. I saw them: two large figures running toward us. It was them, the same kids from the bar. One tall, one short.

They were moving faster now, heads down, shoulders forward, arms out.

I cried out. I yelled. And just as Zeke turned around, the tall man jumped on his back, and wrapped his arms around Zeke's neck and his legs around his waist and dragged him down to the ground. The short man bent over and hit him and kicked him in the face. Zeke struggled and flailed and tried to wrestle free, but the tall one was holding him down still.

I was suspended, frozen— mind-locked and receding further into paralysis.

Janice was backpedaling. She looked at me.

Do something!

The tall man stood up now, and Zeke curled into a fetal position on the ground, still wearing his backpack.

The men were hitting and hitting.

One punched him in the back and the other kicked him and his head bounced on the asphalt.

Go. Do. Something.

Now I felt seized by something outside myself—a libidinal rush, a spasm that passed through my skeleton. And I felt I could not be held accountable for what I was doing. I had the urge to destroy something. I ran forward and jumped up and raised my fist over my head—the way one holds a hammer—and brought it down on the back of his head, knocking him to the ground.

And the tall man turned to face me and shoved me backwards and now—while the men were briefly occupied—Zeke freed himself. He rolled over and staggered to his feet and held himself upright. He moved to stand next to me. Janice stood behind us, yelling, backpedaling still.

And the two men recomposed themselves. They moved in closer, bouncing, the way boxers move before they strike.

Zeke stood unmoved, flatfooted. He was panting. With the back of his wrists, he wiped his mouth, then wiped his wrists against his back pockets. He took off his backpack, reached into it, and pulled something out. A dark little object. At first it looked like a cellphone, but when he rotated the object in his hand and lifted it up into the gritty streetlight, I could see it was a gun. A handgun. He held it up. He pointed it, angled it sideways at the men, who put their hands in the air, as one does in the presence of a police officer.

Do it, Janice said. Fucking do it.

Don't, I said. Please. Don't.

The man yelled something. Zeke told him to shut up. Shut the fuck up. He adjusted his grip on the gun and lifted it to eye level. He shifted his aim from one man to the other, and back to the first. Without taking his eyes off them, he said my name slowly. He said Janice's name and he said my name again. Now he pointed the gun and mumbled something, I don't remember what. He mumbled it again. He mumbled and muttered and moaned. He was moaning and he got louder. He moaned now with the intensity of a power-lifter. Then his grunt turned into a screech or a wail, and he yelled so loudly that, for a moment, I thought someone else had shot him—someone behind a tree or inside a parked car maybe. He yelled so loudly that I yelled, too, and when I yelled, Janice yelled, and soon we were all yelling. All three of us. Yelling and hooting and screeching and wailing and speaking in tongues. In a fit of solidarity, or mimesis, or madness, or thoughtless celebration, we cried out senseless and stupid. We moaned and howled. We made a cacophony of barely human voices: the sound of pain, begging for more pain, afraid or fearless or both. Before long, Zeke was waving the gun loosely around in the air and yelling something else, something new. I started waving my hands in the air, too. I was mimicking him. Janice was doing it, too. Waving her arms and yelling. We looked like lunatic dancers.

Zeke told the men to run home—just as the police officer, weeks earlier, had told me to run.

And they did.

We watched them run, still howling and shrieking and dancing.

My body became suddenly warm. My thoughts slowed down.

Next thing I could tell, we were running, too—sprinting through backyards and alleyways, jumping over gates and piles of trash. Janice took us. She pointed here and there. Now we walked. Now we ran again. Now we were flying—below the freeways and into the foothills and through neighborhoods.

Janice, I said, where are we going?

It's time to disappear again. Are you coming?

PART FIVE

28

Already we were in Janice's dark green Subaru Forester going south on the 5 toward Bakersfield.

The road went down against the arch of the sun and the sky was cloudless—the color of stagnant water. Slowly the trees disappeared, and the expanse of the mountains turned into barren plains, harsh and jagged and wide, a place where other places end, an ancient apocalypse.

We had decided to escape for a week and stay in a hotel outside of Las Vegas. We might as well vacation while we're hiding out, Janice had said.

Janice had invited Zeke to join us, but he said he wasn't scared and that he needed to stay and hold strong and be responsible.

Just before leaving, I had sent all the necessary emails from my phone. I emailed Parker to let him know I wouldn't be at the McDonald's this week, and I emailed the therapist to cancel our appointment. I made something up. I had to leave town suddenly, I said, and tend to a family emergency. I immediately regretted this decision, though, and feared that the therapist would try to reschedule the appointment—that he might be interested in my "family emergency" and want to understand its relationship to my mental health. In the end, it didn't matter. I never saw the therapist again.

For the first time since my accident, my finger felt good. The cut was healed. I took off the bandages. I threw them out.

•

Janice kept the cruise control set exactly at the speed limit—seventy miles per hour, and it felt like we were barely moving, like I'd been looking at the same mountain for the last thirty minutes, the same dirt mounds, the same sagebrush, the same road.

"The Future's Not What It Used to Be" by Mickey Newbury played on the radio.

Why are we listening to this trash? I said.

Janice hit the off button and the car went silent. The tires humming against the hot asphalt.

You don't have to keep it like that, I said. The cruise control. You can legally go up to ten miles over it.

She looked at me and made that lemon-sucking face. Legally?

Legally, yeah.

Then why isn't the speed limit ten miles faster than what it is?

Because then people would drive five or ten miles per hour faster than that limit.

She squinted.

It's not worth it for cops, I said, to pull you over unless you're flying down the highway. At least thirteen miles per hour over the limit. The ticket just isn't worth as much to the city. It's better for them to wait for someone going faster.

In the near distance was a cluster of small buildings—not buildings, but trailers, sheds, U-Haul trucks—above which a tattered American flag rippled in the dry breeze. A hand-written sidewalk sign had been placed by the side of the road. As we approached, I read it aloud: Gas, Liquor, and Grocery. There were other signs, too: ATM. 24 Packs $14.99. Picnic Area in Back.

Janice pulled through the parking lot—a smoothed-over plot of gravel where there were parked two white F-150s with lift kits and an old blue Ford Aerostar. She pulled up so close to the pump that she could not open her door fully without banging it into the concrete pole next to it. She cracked the door and sucked in her stomach and pressed herself through the open crack.

The gas station was a trailer with no windows, a false, rickety structure that looked like a portable classroom. We walked up the moveable steel staircase into the container. The smell was overwhelming. Burning plastic and dust and cold air blowing through an overheating air conditioner.

The words "liquor" and "grocery" on the outdoor sign proved to be a lure, as there was no liquor and no beer even, except for six packs of Bud Light. Two small shelves were thinly stocked with a below-average snack selection: Lays Potato Chips, Flaming Hot Cheetos, Rold Gold Pretzels, Hostess Powdered Mini Donuts, Nature Valley Granola Bars, SlimJims, Grandma's Cookies, Ho Hos, Hot Fries, Chex Mix, and Pringles. There was also a shelf of pre-made food. Frozen burritos, breakfast sandwiches, microwavable cheesy pockets, microwavable hotdogs, Taquitos, yogurt, hard boiled eggs, and cheese sticks with beef jerky.

I thumbed through the frozen food. Do you want anything? I said.

Janice walked over to the shelf and grabbed a Nature Valley bar, two hard-boiled eggs and a cheese stick. I grabbed a frozen burrito and a bag of popcorn.

We approached the cash register.

Can I also get, um, fifty on the pump—what is it—two? Janice said to the cashier.

Fifty on two. The cashier fumbled at the register, pounding the buttons with her index finger, like a blind typist. She couldn't have been older than fifteen years, and she wore an oversized coat that made her look like a floating head. Her dark hair fell to her waist.

Fifty-eight twenty-eight, she said.

Janice handed her the money.

I'm going to heat up this burrito, I said to Janice, but she had already walked out the door. I turned and headed to the back of the trailer where a microwave sat next to a grimy coffee maker.

Actually, I turned around again and walked to the counter, can I have a cup of coffee, too?

The cashier smiled. Her teeth were gray. That's one dollar, she said.

I handed her my credit card.

You got no cash?

No cash, I said.

There's a five-dollar minimum charge.

Never mind, I said. Forget the coffee.

Wait. She reached out, as if to touch me. Just take a cup, she said. It's on me.

I thanked her and went to the back and removed the burrito from its plastic wrapper, soaked a paper towel in the rusted steel sink, wrapped the towel gently around the burrito, set the burrito onto one of the available paper plates, and put it in the microwave for three minutes. During those three minutes, I poured coffee from the cloudy glass pot into a Styrofoam cup and added three packets of Sweet'n Low and three cups of Carnation Half and Half Liquid Creamer and went back outside.

She removed the pump from the gas tank and shut the fuel door. Let's eat this in the picnic area. I hate eating and driving.

Behind the trailer was a combed patch of dirt on which sat two picnic tables beneath a blue canopy. Two families huddled together at the tables. They shared a pack of BudLight—two couples, man and woman, each with one child, two children. Six of them. They halted their conversations and watched us approaching. I wanted to watch them, too, but their eyes outnumbered mine and I couldn't sustain my look. I walked over to a mound of dirt beneath a scrawny desert tree that made no shade and crouched down and brushed away from twigs and small rocks and smoothed out the dust.

I waved Janice over.

We sat on the dirt and ate. Janice looked down at the ground, chewing.

From where I was, I could see the families. The men faced me, and I let myself listen to their conversation:

Joel, said the first man, tell them what you told me yesterday. That's how the first man spoke, in a nasally voice, breathing forcefully out of his mouth. You tell them, said the second man—a scraggly, skinny, rat-looking guy with a cowboy hat and a thin mustache. He spat tobacco into a plastic water bottle, and the spit hit the bottle's rim and trickled down the side into a pool of dark liquid. The man looked too overtly derelict to be so negligent, and I wondered whether and to what degree he'd cultivated that lowlife look.

(Here I wondered, also, whether this might also be true of Janice, the cultivation of a look—whether she had some facade that I failed to notice the first time I met her, and which was too late to notice now.)

The first man nudged the second. Come on, you tell it better, he said.

One of the women reached over and took out a can of beer and cracked it open and poured it slowly into a red plastic cup that she held at an angle, allowing the beer to hit the side of the cup.

Fine. The skinny one spat into the bottle again and smiled in an exaggerated way. He spoke in a reverent voice like he was in the presence of authority. So, me and Robby come out here the other night, he said. And Robby is a mess after the whole deal with Cindy and all that, how she'd been fucking whatshisname, and anyway, we're in his wagon, and he's just shooting shit and he's

got that look in his eye like he's gone do something. I don't know what, but he had that crazy
look, you know, that one he gets when he's been
drinking. And I say, Robby, you've been drinking? He said, my heart's gone, and everything
feels about the same as the day before. And I'm
like, Robby, let me out of this goddamn wagon
right now. He shakes his head like no but his eyes
are still locked onto the road ahead. I'm trying to
calm him down, but he won't have it. He's saying
some crazy shit now like I'm going to kill someone and fuck this and fuck that and fuck it all.

The women were laughing in a way that indicated familiarity.

And I'm starting to freak, he says. This idiot
hits the gas as hard as he can. Just floors the bitch.
So, we're going now, really really going, and thank
god there's no one else on the road because we're
hauling to kill someone. Flying. Off the ground,
it feels like. And I'm looking at the speedometer.
And Mother God, we're going eighty, ninety, a
hundred, one ten.

Now the man lowers his voice even more,
cupping his mouth so the children can't hear. I can
read his lips: I'm screaming my head off, you bas-
tard mutherfucker you're going to kill us! We're
riding like that for God I don't know how long
and finally he slows down and down and down,
and we stop a few miles up the road. I'm not sure
if I should beat his ass or kiss him. And then he
starts laughing like he's psycho. He starts saying
that he thinks he cum'd himself. His pants're wet,
too. Piss and maybe something else too. He said,

243

this is better than getting your dick sucked. I said, what? And he said, better than getting your god-damned dick sucked.

The first man was laughing, but the storyteller was not. He repeated his final sentence again. Better than getting your dick sucked.

•

Back on the road and for a long time nothing to see. No houses. No buildings. Only a procession of cars retreating into the desert. Mountains rose and fell, and new mountains rose to take their place, sun-bleached and bare. There was a primordial monotony to the landscape, a redundancy that made you wonder who you were and what your life meant.

I wanted to ask Janice about Zeke—whether he was her partner—but I didn't want to seem jealous or obsessive, so I let it go. Maybe I wasn't jealous, I thought, and that was a good thing, yeah?

The road dropped down and rose again and wrapped around a dry ravine and through a windgap and straightened out and went flat. Hours and hours. We could see for miles ahead—and because everything was visible, it felt like nothing was. The world seemed hidden. The clouds drifted like dead things in water.

Janice seemed too relaxed, considering what had just happened the night before. She relaxed her shoulders and let them back. She slouched.

Should we talk about last night? I said.

What about it?

It's crazy, right?

No, she said. There's nothing crazy about it. Violence is our life. It's what freedom is supposed to feel like.

The mountains overtook the sun and the sky turned dull white to red, red to blue, blue to blue-turning-black, and the car seemed to float down a dark river.

It was full dark by the time we saw Las Vegas. No stars except the one on the ground, the glowing valley: a pointilated constellation flickering on and off.

The road went down. We exited the 95 onto the 215, took it to Charleston, and drove west until Charleston became the 159, and led us to a small town in a valley nested between a cluster of red mountains.

When we got into town, the sight of an illuminated strip mall was enough to make me cry. It was as ordinary as any strip mall I'd seen before, lined with the most generic establishments: Great Clips, Dollar Tree, Subway, Euro Tanning Salon, Hobby Lobby and a standalone Starbucks in the parking lot. As soon as I saw it, I started to weep. Humiliated, ashamed, confused, I turned my head to the side and moved closer to the window. I watched myself crying, reflected against the glass, superimposed against the fictional city behind it—into and out of the linked streetlights, so that my image was visible and invisible as we passed from dark to light, then dark again. We went into Las Vegas—past the sprawl of identical housing developments, and more stucco strip malls, past the keno lounges and the golf courses—and then out again.

We drove back into the primitive landscape of rocks and sand and shrubs, into what felt like the future, barren and empty.

Now the car slowed on the dirt road and the tires crunched against the gravel. Janice turned onto a driveway pulled up a little farther and slowed down and stopped and turned the car off. The keys hung from the ignition and rattled.

We're here, she said.

Where?

29

The hotel was different from the places we usually went. It was a serious place, a real place, a
place where people go to be in love.

Our room was practically two rooms. The
walls were thick adobe. A desert aesthetic. There
were exotic plants that looked like light fixtures
and light fixtures that looked like exotic plants.
There was a painting of the desert next to a giant
window looking out onto a view of the same desert. On the table, there was a large wooden bowl
with fruit inside. I focused on it. Even here—in
what felt like a palace or paradise—there were
these grotesquely long, green grapes, a withered
banana, shrunken mangos and peaches. I saw it
as a kind of still life—the banana was the sickly
brain, and the grapes were the impotent genitals.
There was something surreal about it, something
repulsive and sickening. I thought about the exhibit of abject art at SFMOMA—the bodies and
shit and vomit. I wondered what it meant that ordinary fruit was like abject art. Probably nothing.

Janice unpacked her suitcase. She took out a
pile of clothes and began throwing them into the
air, one by one, which lost their shape as they fell
lifeless onto the floor in a heap of disorder—faux
fur vests, zig zag leggings, bright crop tops, sweat
pants, tie-dye tank tops. She threw everything
out until her suitcase was completely empty and
then she got on her knees and began throwing the

clothes all over again, tossing them up to create a mess.

What are you doing?

Try it, she said. Make yourself at home.

I tried it. I went to my backpack and took out my clothes and threw them around. I threw my jeans onto the television. I threw my shirts onto the floor and my socks onto the dresser.

Feels good, right?

Feels great.

Janice took off the clothes she was wearing and turned on the shower and invited me to join her and I did and after the shower we fooled around and sat in place for a long time.

Janice propped herself up on her forearms and elbows. She tilted her neck back so that her face was pointed at the ceiling. The overhead lights reflected against her black hair and her sweaty skin.

Maybe I was swept up in the moment, but now was the first time I had the thought: Maybe I am in love with her.

I didn't say that out loud.

•

Janice slept in. I woke and had some time alone. I went down to the lobby to have breakfast. I drank two cups of coffee and ate toast and fruit. I took out my phone and checked the news. Local news and national news and whatever else passed for a credible source of information, the *Daily Californian* and the *New York Times* and the *UC Police Re-*

port, everything—to see whether there had been any reports about guns, fights, protests, riots, civil unrest, Antifa. Anything. As far as the internet was concerned, there were no such events.

I went upstairs and turned off my phone and hid it in a drawer. The sun was up now, and the room was so bright that I wanted Janice to see it. A romantic gesture, I thought. I woke her up and said, look, look at the light! And she rolled toward me and grabbed a pillow and swung it and hit me upside the head and said, I'm on vacation, goddamnit.

•

For days, Janice and I enjoyed a version of monogamy. We never left the hotel. We swam in the pool and napped in the sun and swam again. We sunbathed on the balcony. We drank coffee in the morning and wine in the afternoon. We ate fresh salad with goat cheese and beets and bread with butter and honey, and we read books. Books! I read a book for the first time in—how long? Years, maybe. *Don Quixote.* The hotel had a copy. Janice read something, too—something about mythology and psychology and the "failed absolute," whatever that was. We talked about what we read. (I still didn't understand what the "failed absolute" was.) Janice told stories. She told a story about her first polyamorous partner—a white guy with a thirteen-inch cock. Thirteen inches, she said again, when it was limp. Limp! It was too big, she said. We couldn't even have sex because it wouldn't fit. Not even in my mouth. I had to use both hands on him. He believed God had cursed him—played a sick joke on him so that his gift was also his curse. A gift so great that it became a form of torture. Some nights he cried over his huge penis. Was she making this up? It didn't matter. I laughed the whole time. I asked her to tell more stories and she did. She told me a story—about the first time she came to San Francisco—how she got drunk and stoned and got lost on Valencia—how she loved that feeling. Being lost. How she missed that feeling these days, how she had been trying to recreate it for years. She told me about getting her first tattoo. She told me about her first gay encounter (her words) which had been a failure because, halfway through it, her partner asked her to stop. Why? She was too embarrassed to ask. Hilarious. We played board games and watched black and white films and listened to music. We touched each other's faces and hands. You have these freckles, I said. You have that crooked nose, she said. You're adventurous. You're easy-going. You're outspoken. You're pious. Pious? Like, you could have been an old Catholic. A monk, or something. Don't deny it.

It felt like we were hiding out—escaping the tedium and banality of our lives. Everything was easy. I had nothing to pretend. And I felt, for the first time since graduate school, a sense of freedom and openness. I listened to the breeze. I felt sweat running down my forehead. I unburdened by thoughts except to think about how I wasn't overthinking. Maybe I was experiencing what a saint might call an *epiphany*, or a therapist might call *recovering*, or a writer might call *character development*, though, for once, the language of experience did not prevent me from experiencing what the language meant.

The sky was empty, and the sun was up, and no shadows fell. We went to the pool again, drank wine again, and read our books. I watched Janice as she fiddled with the bottom button of her sundress, her fingernails clicked softly against it.

This is our sexcapade, she said.

Let's never go back.

Let's move to Las Vegas and become pornstars.

Sure, I said, why not?

Do you think you could do it?

Porn? No.

No?

No way.

Why not?

I'm too small.

Some guys like to watch porn with small cocks, she said. It's good for their self-esteem.

Okay.

So, *would* you do it?

Would *you*?

Why not?

I don't know. There's the whole staged aspect of it. I can't get over that. I spent too much of my life feeling like I'm being watched.

Watched?

God or Google. Always watching me.

I like the project of porn, she said.

The project?

I think about those sappy movies about love and sorrow, those dramas and corny romantic comedies about close relationships and personal experience. Those are more scandalous than porn. Porn is a kind of censorship, if you think about it. What's censored in porn is the personal narrative. Feelings. Porn censors out human feelings. The way people used to flash their tits and dicks, now they flash their feelings.

Yeah.

It's disgusting.

This was one of the best things about Janice. Top five. I never knew when she was serious, when she was kidding. Was she kidding now?

We went on like that for hours talking and saying things we didn't necessarily believe, or used to believe, or might believe in the future. We joked about buying a virtual yacht in the metaverse. About writing erotic novels and releasing them as NFTs. About the return of Victorian sexual codes disguised as hyper-specific, new-age sexual orientations. About starting an unironic OnlyFans page for men to look at other men's small cocks and feel better about themselves. Average Joes. Joe's Average. Tiny's Tim.

•

And then something changed.

I made a mistake.

It was night. Late. I had just finished and then Janice finished, and we looked at each other.

I made a face, although I can't say what the face was or what it meant. I didn't mean to make it, but I knew I had because, when I did, Janice's eyebrows flared up like tiny bat wings. Her freckles were bright, more visible and numerous than usual because we'd been in the sun so much. She stood up and looked at herself in the mirror for a long time and then turned back to me and said, you love me.

She said it just like that. You love me.

I do?

I can tell, she said. I can tell by the way you look at me. Like that. That way. Like the world is ending.

Why are you saying this?

See, she said. See? That's it. That look.

What look?

That look. Like that.

This is just my face, I said. See?

She paced the room, possessed by a sudden intensity, and then walked into the bathroom. I didn't know what to do or where to go, so I didn't go anywhere. A few minutes later, she came out again and sat down at the edge of the bed and took her phone out of her pocket and began to scroll with the middle finger. You're too deep now, she said. You want to get inside me. All the way inside. You think your cock is more than your cock.

What are you talking about?

You think your cock is a metaphor or something.

The hell?

But it's not. It's just a cock.

She stood up again and started getting ready for bed. She put on her sweatpants and started washing her face.

I'm going to read in the lobby, I said.

She nodded and made a face like she was sucking a lemon and said, I'm going to bed.

30

I walked through the lobby and went into the pool which was lit up by underwater lights and sat on a lounge chair and read my *Quixote*. I wasn't reading the novel in any linear kind of way. I jumped around from episode to episode, settling here and there when I felt inclined to do so, hoping to find something useful or moving. I was struck by a certain scene. I read it twice. It went like this.

Quixote sends Sancho off to deliver a letter to his lover, Dulcinea. Sancho knows his task is impossible because Dulcinea is an illusion of Quixote's chivalric imagination. She is a fantasy. The very center of Quixote's entire worldview. This is why Dulcinea matters most. She is the god of love or desire or passion. But she is the most real of Quixote's illusions because he will never find her. She both exists and does not exist.

How will Sancho deliver the letter to Dulcinea without ruining Quixote's vision of her?

Now, here come three peasant women riding by on donkeys.

Sancho rushes to tell Quixote that Dulcinea is coming. Look.

No, says Quixote. Those are peasants on donkeys. None is Dulcinea.

Sancho falls on his knees before one of the women. He praises her beauty and glory and fame. We have found Dulcinea!

Quixote is confused. Dulciana—now he

sees her—is repulsive. She stinks. She's dirty. Quixote's fantasy is on the verge of collapse—his worldview threatens to fall apart.

But here Sancho intervenes. This *is* Dulcinea, he insists. She is beautiful, but her beauty has been obstructed by a dark magic that seeks to delay your satisfaction. You cannot see her because the universe does not want her to be seen. But I assure you, Sir, this is your Lady.

The scene is profound as it is comedic. What struck me was that Sancho's intervention is not pathetic or condescending. His intervention is heroic. He intuitively understands that Don Quixote is not insane, but he entertains a useful delusion. A delusion that gives his life a purpose. And although, at the end of the novel, Quixote does eventually lose his fantasy—and although the loss of that fantasy initiates his metaphoric and literal death—Sancho is, in this moment, I thought, the novel's unironic hero.

31

Next morning, we ate breakfast on the patio and went swimming and read our books and didn't talk much. The sunlight made it hard to see, and I couldn't keep my eyes open.

Janice had an idea.

What is it?

Want to spend our last day in the city?

The city?

Las Vegas. We could go downtown and check out the bars and whatever. We could stay on Fremont Street.

I wondered whether her idea to change hotels had anything to do with the previous night.

•

Now the windows were down, and I was driving, and Janice was fumbling with the radio dial. Now she stopped fumbling. She turned up the volume. Country music blasted from the speakers.

I reached down to change the station, but Janice slapped my hand away. Then she rolled down her window and her hair blew everywhere and briefly she had no face.

The Subaru pushed through the winding roads and the city rose out of the valley and sprawled out across the desert. The sky was big, pocked with long thin clouds and drifted against our driving.

I parked the car where she told me to park it, near a row of old shipping containers: brick, characterless factory-type structures which had been transformed into breweries, bars, and boutique restaurants in a gentrification effort disguised— Janice told me—as a revitalization project. From the parking garage, we checked into our hotel, the Golden Spike (motel style, the kind we visited in the East Bay) and threw down our bags and went out again.

We walked southwest along Las Vegas Boulevard, surrounded by a barrage of images—billboards and lights, advertisements for law firms and local political candidates and strip clubs— half-naked women and old men. The sunlight fell crimson across the valley and the desert appeared to burn. Red mountains rose in the distance beyond the intersection of highways and a faint moon materialized into view. We ate lunch at a cheap buffet, for the experience, not the food. It's an experience, Janice said. A real Vegas buffet. And we loaded our trays with way more food than one could possibly eat—baked potatoes, steak, pepperoni pizza, enchiladas, Chow Mein, French fries, fried bananas, soft-serve ice cream, and Pad Thai (which, yeah, I did not eat). Every cuisine was represented, anything one might be craving.

When we were finished and full and done, we threw what was left away. And we went again and wandered up and down the casino floors at the Golden Nugget and the D and the California and the Golden Gate—a horizontal spiral of mirrors and staining lights, where each new space felt like a further disappearance, where each room was nearly identical to the one before it, fast food courts, rows of slot machines, nightclubs, poker tables, bowling alleys and lobby entrances. We watched sad gamblers as they mindlessly pulled and pushed at the slot machines, and I watched the cocktail waitresses, middle aged women clad in tight-fitting dresses, and the drunkards stumbling their way through the lobby, worn out, almost sleeping.

Fremont Street is where the music was. We walked beneath the giant canopy ceiling that spanned the length of an entire block. A light show was in progress and the screen-sky flashed with geometric shapes and digital fireworks, choreographed to the rock and rap and country music playing too loudly from the surrounding, oversized speakers disguised as gigantic rocks or treasure boxes. For a moment, everyone, all of us, paused and looked up, shock still in awe or boredom, as if before some great, stupid god.

Janice's face was washed with light.

This was the historic version of the myth of Las Vegas, anachronistically futuristic. The streets were lined with revitalized images from the glittery 1940's and 50s, the Vegas of Elvis and Frank Sinatra and the Golden Nugget. The old neon signs were back and lit up in augmented reality: the Golden Spike, Chinese Lucky Cat, Lucky Lady, the revolving Ruby Slipper, Binion's giant horseshoe, the crouching cowgirl, Vegas Vic and his pot of gold. I was overwhelmed by a sense of nostalgia for a past I never knew—a world that never belonged to me, a lost future.

We stopped to get a few drinks and talked about the "mole people"—a desperate community of hundreds living in flood tunnels directly below the Las Vegas Strip. We went to another bar and then another. Janice posted a photo of her drink on Instagram. She tweeted something. We walked again, swept in by the carnival of Fremont Street, past the live bands and the street performers and "midget orchestra" and the Nude guitarist and the whole cast of adult characters—the Tarzan lookalike, the Old-Vegas showgirls, totally nude except for the huge feather headdresses and gold stars covering their nipples and crotch area. There was a fat man in a giant baby mask. There were two men dressed in Mario Brothers costumes with a Vegas twist: holding beer bottles and heroine needles. A homeless man held a cardboard box over his head on which he had written "Fuck You." Two men dressed up like Jedi Knights fought each other with plastic lightsabers. Two women dressed in devil costumes—with red sequin dresses, horns, arrow-headed tails—who, they said, would whip me for a small fee. And for a small fee, three women dressed like angels in white thongs, would let me take a photo. I walked past kiosks selling faux-silk scarves, cellulite cellphone accessories, Mardi Gras beads, disco ball necklaces, and bobbleheads of famous politicians; past the street bars and the bar carts and the ABC stores selling mostly alcohol; past the sale reps, who lured passersby into their nightclubs and strip clubs with discount cards; past more half-naked people, dancing drunk in the street—kissing and fondling each other's private parts; past Heart Attack Grill where patrons over three hundred and fifty pounds were promised a free meal; past sleazy bars and lounges; past the dark shopping malls, the giant metal sculpture of a praying mantis that blew fire from its antennae; past the "interactive pop-up experience" and its papier-mâché polar bear sculptures made for taking Instagram photos with. The whole history of human civilization was there and not there at once in the plastic models of Rome and Paris and Venice and Dubai.

We headed back to the hotel and sat for a while, but soon it was late. Janice was getting ready for bed. Sweatpants and all that. She was brushing her teeth already, something she usually did after sex. Toothpaste foamed around her lips. She spit into the sink and a line of toothpaste ran down her chin.

A green light poured in through the window, a faux-neon sign that blinked on and off, so that our room went light then dark again.

I felt suddenly agitated and restless and knew I wouldn't sleep. I scrolled through my phone in a frantic, annoyed kind of way.

I'm going back out, I said.

Now? You're going out now? (Because her mouth was full of toothpaste, it sounded more like "wow.") She brushed furiously, scrubbing her gums and tongue, faster. She shoved the toothbrush down her throat and gagged. She spit.

Toothpaste ran down her chin.

Legs are restless, I said. I need to keep moving.

Sure, she said. Okay.

32

I shared the elevator down with a leathery guy in a white cowboy hat. He wore a Canadian tuxedo, holes in his denim jacket. A tobacco-stained mustache. He leaned against the side of the elevator and, rejecting conventional elevator etiquette, faced me. He handled his star-shaped belt buckle and smacked his lips and flicked his tongue against his teeth. With both hands, he reached into his back pocket, removed a small black comb, and stroked his mustache with it. He was still looking at me. He took off his hat and scratched his head. He sighed and cleared his throat like he was about to speak. He put his hands in his pocket and seemed to fiddle with himself through it.

"Happiness is a Warm Gun" played on the speakers.

Outside, I walked away from the lights, through the little side streets and back allies, down one byway and another and another.

My face was still numb from all the alcohol. I found a small bar and went in. I didn't feel like drinking. Didn't feel like much of anything, but had nothing else to do.

Inside was red. The décor, all of it. The walls were covered with velvet crimson curtains. Four booths. Upholstered red. The carpet was a disorienting zigzag pattern.

The place was empty save three drunks at the bar. One couple—woman and man who sat at the front, nearer the entrance, and a man hunched over his drink toward the back. No music played and I heard my own footsteps, awkward and uneven. I sat in the middle.

The bartender was there. A young woman, all bones. Her arms were covered in nondescript tattoos that looked more like bruises than anything else, blotches of purple and grey. Maybe an elephant? Maybe a jellyfish? It tangled itself in knots around her shoulders.

Whiskey with ice, and a seltzer water, please and thank you.

She lifted her chin and tossed a napkin in front of me and took the scoop shovel and held it loosely—keeping her fingers straight, wrapping her thumb around the handle, pressing it into her palm—and from the freezer lifted more ice than seemed necessary and dumped it into a tumbler.

Local? she said.

Me? Not really.

She poured the whiskey and set the glass in front of me and drew a rag from her pocket and wiped circles on the surface of the bar. Whereabouts?

San Francisco area.

She shook her head. I don't know why y'all leave California to come out here. If I could get out, I'd never leave. Fuck, I'd walk there if I could afford to stay.

I drank and looked around—there were plush velvet couches, cherry wood chairs and tables and a faux fireplace in the corner.

The couple at the end of the bar stood up

and stumbled their way out of the bar, laughing about something.

I'm not here on vacation, I said.

She hummed and continued polishing the bar. Business?

Research.

Research.

Huh.

I'm trying to write a novel, I said. But I don't have a story.

She blew air out of her nose, imitating laughter.

The silence—absence of music—seemed to be growing louder.

Now the man to my right moved over several seats, laboring, and sat next to me. He hunched over the bar and rested on his elbows and looked me up and down and took a drink from his glass. He wore a fedora and a blue and yellow Tommy Bahamas button-up. An unlit cigarette hung loosely in the corner of his mouth. Sorry, he said. Don't mean to bother.

I nodded.

You say you're a writer, is at right?

I nodded.

He could have been a used-car-salesman, smiling with half of his mouth to keep the other half firmly clenched down on his cigarette. Perfect, he said. I've been looking for one of those. A writer. I have a good story to tell. It's a great story. Maybe you'll want to write it.

His breath was a mild rot. He produced a lighter from his pocket and lit up his cigarette. It's a good story, he said again. People need to hear it.

Tell it.

What, now?

Sure.

He puffed his cigarette and blew smoke in my direction. The smoke lingered and covered his face in a coil of haze. I'm Benici, he said.

Okay, Benici.

Yeah, he said. It's Italian, I think.

I said my name and shook his hand. His skin felt taut like an over-inflated balloon.

The bartender leaned against the bar and folded her arms.

It goes like this, said Benici. I had this friend, let's call him Joe. He's a freckled boy. Dark hair. He played baseball in high school. And he's okay, too. Not great, but okay. And he's sad. He's sad all the time. But doesn't know why. As an adult, he's drugged up day and night. Anti-pain drugs and antidepressants. And he has one blue eye. Just one.

Is that a metaphor or something?

Is what a what?

The eye.

You're asking me if the eye is a metaphor?

The blue one. The single blue eye.

This is a true story I'm telling.

If we're going to write this story, Joe can't just happen to have one eye.

In this story, you hear me, everything is exactly what it is, and nothing else.

I thought about that.

But things only become themselves in relation to other things, I said.

I'm not trying to make some statement. A thing is a thing.

I gestured for him to continue.

Joe, let me say from the start, is the devil. Satan himself. Lucifer. Beelzebub. One night, he's drunk and coked-up and he's speaking unintelligibly about this or that. Mostly he's ranting about the Dodgers, how they've blown the world series two years in a row. I should've mentioned that. That's where the book must begin, if you choose to write it. The devil loves the Dodgers. There's your opening line. Anyway, I say to him, Joe, I say, you're acting like the devil. And he looked at me all serious and he says, I am the devil, boy. And from then on, it was like the sun was shining on him, and I could see him—the devil.

I don't understand, what makes him the devil?

Ben paused and rubbed his chin. Lots, he said. So much. For one thing, he buys cigarettes for children and all that. He sells meth to his cousins. That type of deal. Also, he has voices in his head. Sick voices.

I know a guy like that, I said.

One day, Joe wakes in the middle of the night, he said, and walks to the bathroom to piss. But he can't piss. He stands there and pushes and pushes, but nothing. He can't pee. His stomach cramps and he wants to vomit. He tries to go back to sleep, but it doesn't work. He can't piss. Hours pass. By morning, he starts drinking and drinking

water. More and more of it. Finally, he goes outside and stands in the front lawn and does it. He
releases everything. And as he's pissing, he says
out loud, as if there's someone there with him,
Thank God. And it occurs to him that this has
been the purpose of his life—to reach the end of
something. He realizes—he told me this, keep in
mind, these are his words—that he is only ever
in pursuit of ends, ends in themselves. Goals. But
there's never an end to end-seeking, and he per-
petually seeks the end to what never ends. He's
telling me all this one afternoon, drunk by the
pool. He grabs his cellphone, like this, and holds
it up to the light, and says, this has no past. He
said it just like that. This has no past. This is our
uniform and our body. I tell him to shut the fuck
up, I say you're drunk and talking like a donkey.
He says, if we all have the same body, then our
body does not belong to us, and the only way
to differentiate the body is to mark it. Cut it up,
he says. Scar it. Disfigure it to reclaim whatever
it was. And that was that. Three days later the
devil kills himself, alone in a motel room, somewhere in Carson City, hopped up on fentanyl and
heroine and cocaine and rum and whatever else.
He shoots the devil right in the face. Square in
the middle, where the brain used to be. No more
brain. No more head. Poor fuck. I don't know why
he did it. I don't think he knew why he did it. He's
tired of being the devil, I guess. But you see where
I'm headed. The devil isn't dead. The devil is well
and breathing. The story is what takes place after he kills himself. This is a true story, mind you.

Every word. After Joe kills himself, one of his friends kills himself, too. And then another. All these men are killing themselves.

What men?

It doesn't matter. You don't know them anyway. Point is, Joe's life and his death had aftereffects. Unintended results. The end of Joe for him was not the end of him for those who knew him. Even in death he couldn't end it. Your life doesn't belong to you.

How does it end?

Well, he grinned. The Dodgers win the world series.

The Dodgers?

Didn't you see it? It just happened. The Dodgers just won the world series, don't you pay attention?

The Dodgers.

Joe was always bitching about the Dodgers. If he had waited one more season, he'd've seen it. The Dodgers. His beloved Dodgers. And they came good, the Dodgers, the Dodgers.

Okay, I said. The Dodgers.

There's your story for you.

And that was it. Just like that. He was done talking now. He took his wallet from his coat pocket, removed a wad of cash, much more than would have been necessary to cover for a few drinks and a tip, threw it down on the bar, and shook my hand, and told me good luck, and nodded, and walked out.

The bartender and I made eye contact. She paced and then stood on the opposite end of the bar and leaned her hip into it and started to polish glasses.

I sat for a while and tried to think.

What do you make of that story? I asked.

She shrugged and said don't take him too seriously, and went on stacking the glasses. When she was finished, she stood upright again and looked down at her phone.

Hey, I said, why don't you play music here?

She walked over to me. This is how a bar is supposed to be, she said. No music. Only the sound of human interaction.

What if there's no interaction?

Then there's nothing to hear.

•

The lights were off when I got back to the hotel room. I changed into my sweatpants and crawled into bed without brushing my teeth and rolled over three or four times to get comfortable. Janice turned toward me, half-awake. She reached down and grabbed my hand and pulled it into her crotch and placed my finger against her clitoris. Now she pressed her finger into mine so that her hand dictated how I touched her, and she fingered herself with my finger. Faster and slower and faster. Now she exhaled dramatically and rolled away.

In that bare hotel room, I hovered around sleep, never quite reaching it. I turned side to side, overcome by the onset of a quietude that seemed inherent to a place like that. The sign outside our window blinked on and off. EXIT. It made the whole room green. Even when I closed my eyes, I could still see it.

PART SIX

33

When we got back to California, a forest fire was burning in the hills. It happened, they said, because the soil moisture was totally depleted in that part of California; or because unusually warm temperatures dried out the vegetation, making it prone combustion; or because of greenhouse gas emissions and the accompanying dying landscape; or because of unattended campfires and equipment malfunctions and negligently discarded cigarettes and unruly engine sparks and gender reveal parties; or because every time we fought a fire in the past, we inadvertently preserved a heap of burnable vegetation that nature or God intended to burn.

For days the fire tore through the mountains from Grizzly Peak to William Rust and our streets were glazed with an overlay of gray, a grainy film. Smoke settled the valley and the Bay, and ash fell like rain. The sky was sick—an alien color, orange and crimson. And from anywhere in town, one could hear a cacophony of ordinary life that reverberated through the crowded streets and alleyways and coffee shops. A countdown. Drilling and hammering and breaking down; combustion and mechanical equipment; jackhammers and wheel tractors and bulldozers and cars and trucks. Scaffolding protruded here and there. Everywhere was the noise, a buzzing of thermal energy, pure matter and material, building or rebuilding, renovating and remodeling and casual haste: the wiry textures of systematizing and assemblage and erection.

It was November. All things were coming to an end, but not yet.

I spent my time thinking about Janice, wishing to replicate or solidify what happened in the desert. She didn't call. She didn't text unless I texted first. In time, I saw her less and less.

ME: today is my day, right?
JANICE: my work schedule is changing
ME: okay
ME: i'm free anytime
ME: tomorrow?

•

The phone kept going. *A cathedral was bombed in Italy. A school was bombed in Ireland. Several dissenters were hanged in Pakistan. A right-wing candidate was attacked at his first campaign rally in France. A volcano destroyed several villages in Indonesia. Russian troops gathered at the Ukrainian border. The US carried out an airstrike against an Iranian-backed militia in Syria. Surging refugee numbers in Syria led to a spike in terrorism. Thousands of Sudanese took to the streets in the capital of Khartoum to protest a recent military coup.*

In the desert, I hadn't thought once about the presidential election, but as soon as we were home—if I could call Berkeley home—it was thrust into my brain. I couldn't not think about it. I watched the final presidential debate: Candidate A accused Candidate B of trying to start a war to get reelected. Candidate A said: Iran appears to be standing down. And then: No Americans were harmed. Candidate B said: We need a *new* new deal, and if we don't get one the future of our planet is in jeopardy; in ten years, certain parts of our planet will be unsustainable. Candidate A said: We're looking at sinks and showers and other bathroom regulations. Some people are turning on the faucet and they don't get any water. People turn on their showers and water comes trickling out. People are flushing the toilet ten times, fifteen times. They end up using more water than they would otherwise. These new light bulbs, have you seen them? They don't work as well as the old ones. They're more expensive, people can't even afford them. With his pointer finger he pointed at the pulpit. Then he raised both arms in the air and, holding his hands above his head, imitated a lightbulb flickering with his fingers. Candidate B said, We need not fear the future. Candidate A said. It's not the future we fear, but that we won't make it there. That there won't be any future. Candidate B said, We need not fear machines of tomorrow. We should see the purpose of machines as a human purpose. Their project is our project.

In Berkeley, we were invested in making sure our candidate won. And so, by myself, I continued attending the rallies, the protests, the walk outs, the marches and whatever else people were calling them. Both celebration and lamentation.

Monday was the march down Telegraph. Tuesday was the occupation of Sproul Hall. Friday was the Sheraton Palace demonstration. Wednesday, the march down Bancroft. Saturday, the campus police shut down the student radio station. Sunday, a confrontation between the free speech rally and the rally against hate at Saint Mark's Episcopal Church. Monday, the rally against hate, again. Thursday, the "refuse fascism" rally. Friday, a march on campus. Saturday, a march against provocation. On Monday, the news reported damaged property at Gap, Starbucks, McDonald's (not my McDonald's), and other corporate properties. We marched for justice, equality, the end of war, economic freedom. Power in numbers. The streets were loud and teeming with cops. Crowds gathered and sprawled out across the streets and moved as a collective body, a hive mind, a giant first-person plural. I wore my tote bag tightly around my arm. I wore black. I admit, it was easy enough for me to go. Work had slowed down and my motivation was as much social as it was political. I wanted to do the right thing, of course, but also, I wanted to be around people.

Most of all, I wanted to run into Janice or Zeke or, even Julio.

But I did not.

•

On what was supposed to be one of my days with Janice, Parker texted me about a house party and—since I hadn't heard from Janice—I went.

I had planned to get there early, to see Parker, catch up, and leave before a crowd had gathered, but the house was already full of people I didn't recognize. I walked around the living room, dodging, shifting from one side to the other, half-dancing to the music. I went into the kitchen and recognized Khushal from the previous party. He saw me, too—gave me a head nod and returned to his conversation.

Have you seen Parker? I asked him, but he didn't hear me or pretended not to.

I opened the refrigerator and crouched down as if looking for something. There was a twenty-four pack of cheap beer, and I reached into the box and grabbed a can, cracked it, and stood in the corner and sipped and looked at the phone to hide my face.

I texted Parker to tell him I was here and then walked into the backyard and then, right there (I don't know why the possibility hadn't occurred to me before), I saw Janice, sitting alone in a lounge patio chair, facing away.

My jaw clenched shut.

Instantly I resented that Janice hadn't invited me to the party. I knew she often went to parties without telling me. She did almost everything without telling me. I knew—of course, I did—that we were only partners, that she had other lives, lives to which I was not granted access.

We are entitled to other lives, she'd said.

Just then, two men approached and spoke to her. Two men. Both older than us, I thought, her and me. One of the men—the taller one, gym-goer, I guessed, with a mildly receding hairline—put his hand on Janice's forehead, as if to check her temperature. They laughed, the three of them. And the other man—shorter, scruffy, bearded, dressed in leather sandals—sat and made a pouty face, and stuck his lip out.

I didn't want to think about what was going on, how they all knew each other, but I couldn't stop it. They are her ex-lovers, new lovers, future lovers. She knew them from long ago, when Janice was first testing out polyamory. Look at them, how open they seem with each other, the casual intimacy, the natural volume of their words.

The backyard was illuminated only by the dim kitchen light, and in that residual glow, everything and everyone seemed to move in slow motion.

I sat on an empty lawn chair and looked at my phone: still nothing from Parker.

Should I go to Janice? Should I wait for the men to leave?

The light was moving. The people were moving in it. I tried to tune myself to the kitchen conversations but couldn't make out the words. A wave of meaningless noise.

Now the two men were saying goodbye. The taller kissed Janice on the forehead. And she stood and hugged them longer than seemed necessary.

I could see now that she had a bottle of wine. She held it up and seemed to offer the men a drink; and, when they refused, she thrust the bottle up to her mouth, almost play acting, and locked her lips around the rim and threw back her head to let the wine go down.

I remembered my first night with her. I thought about how our then-potential relationship had turned into an actual one—about how the gap between potential and actual had widened, continued to widen.

Okay. Now Janice was alone.

I walked up to her and put my arm on her shoulder. I said hello. Hi. She tensed and turned around. Her face hardened. Hey, she mouthed the word without saying it. She crossed her arms like she was covering herself up. She cleared her throat and looked up at me and raised her eyebrows.

I asked if she was okay.

Bad move. She didn't like that.

She leaned into the chair and closed her eyes. She exhaled to communicate—I don't know what—annoyance, maybe.

I pulled up a chair next to her and sat. The chair was flimsy and unstable, and I nearly fell off and struggled to right myself.

Did I do something wrong?

Not everything is about you, she said. She sounded different. Her voice was deeper. She dragged out her vowels.

Just then, my name. Someone said my name.

The voice was Parker's. He said Janice's name, too. He smiled and rubbed his hands together and touched me. Janice acted happy to see him, I knew she was pretending. I knew that smile: too many teeth showing.

Janice stood and said she needed to go to the bathroom. I'll be right back, she said. She took the green bottle with her, and that's how I knew she wasn't coming back.

I watched her go.

Parker was watching me watch her. He reeked of whiskey.

What the hell was that about? he said.

What?

That. Whatever just happened.

I shrugged. Do you have any more of that whiskey?

He reached into his backpack and pulled out a bottle, twisted off the lid and handed it to me.

Answer the question, he said.

I drank. What question?

That, he said again. That, with Janice. That whole thing.

I don't know.

Are you guys dating?

She doesn't date, I said.

I know she doesn't date. You clown. Have you been hooking up with her? Did you sleep with her?

I couldn't decipher his tone—was he upset? Had he also been sleeping with her? Had he slept with her? Or wanted to?

Yeah, I said. Yeah, so what?

You fucked up, he grinned. You should have told me. I could've warned you.

I'm in love with her, I guess.

You guess.

I don't know.

Parker made the sound a pig makes right before you feed it. She's poly, you know.

I know she's poly.

She's a yes-sayer. Yes to a world of yeses. Is that what you want?

I don't know, sure. Why not?

Yes is the consumer's mantra? Yes yes yes.

Shut up.

Desire is an outward swinging door, he said.

I don't know what that means.

All we desire is more desire.

Okay.

We moved on to other subjects. We talked about social awkwardness and distraction and spectacle. We talked about writing and I admitted that I wasn't writing, and he admitted that he wasn't writing either.

We should be writing right now, I said.

Fuck that.

We're failures, I said.

Who cares, he said. We chose this life. It's more Romantic to be a failure, anyway. A starving artist who dies alone in obscurity. Sign me up for that.

We talked about how our lives were getting smaller and smaller and soon, very soon, they would be too small for us to do anything about it. That's what Parker said. He said, Soon, our lives will be so small we won't be able to see outside them.

Finally, we talked about going home, and

how lame it was to go home before it was even dark, and then—when there wasn't anything else to talk about—we did go home, each our own way.

34

The curtains were shut and the wind was blowing and the evening sunlight was on the floor.

Someone knocked on the glass.

I leapt up and, when I looked, Janice was there—her dark silhouette shifted and shuffled past the frame, and I went to the window and drew back the curtain and pointed to the front door.

Front door, I said. Come in.

She walked away and now I worried that she had interpreted my gesture as a negative one, and that she had read my lips incorrectly, go home maybe, or get out. I reached for my phone and called her. I heard her phone ring as she walked into the room.

Did you just call me?

Sorry, never mind.

I took in Janice's appearance, noting possible differences in her demeanor or attire—anything to clue me into what she wasn't telling me. She wore slacks and heels, what one might wear to an event, and I worried that she was setting a formal tone for whatever was happening, or about to happen.

She took off her shoes. You look like you're about to cry, she said.

And I did cry. I threw my arms around her.

You're suffocating me, she said. Dude, you're suffocating me.

I apologized and told her I was happy to see her—that I'd had a few miserable days, that I missed her, that I'd been thinking about Las Vegas, that I hadn't slept well and that I'd gotten wasted the night before and that my head was foggy, that I'd been attending rallies and events. I put my hand around my throat, as if attending to pain. I told her that maybe I did love her, and so what. I wasn't afraid of that.

By now, the sunlight was gone. Janice's hair seemed darker than usual. It fell into her eyes.

Why wasn't she responding?

Aren't you going to say something?

Nothing. Now she leaned over and kissed me. She breathed deeply and said okay, okay, okay. She reiterated to me how she didn't believe in romantic love—only physical need. Only need and sex. Love, or whatever you want to call it, is not a biological reality.

What is with you and biology?

I believe in science.

Okay.

Look it up. Love is like religion or something. The opium of the masses. Make us feel better about how sad and boring our lives are. But also makes us dumb. It's fiction, love is.

As I listened—Oh—I remembered something. Quixote and Sancho. Which one am I? Here comes Dulcinea riding her horse.

Okay, I said. Maybe. But everyone needs a fiction. Nothing works unless you buy into the fantasy of the thing. You have to believe in something before you can see it. My voice went up now and I felt that for the first time in a long time I was saying what I wanted to say. I think you're scared, I said. That's all.

Janice's arms were crossed. She said my name. She said it again. And then, after a long silence, she spoke to me the way one speaks to a child, the way one breaks news of tragedy. Maybe you're right, she said. But it is an ancient truth that to love another is to die. To lose the life you have. And in the future, there is no need for love.

The future? What do you know about the future?

Soon life extension will be possible, and we'll be living for hundreds of years. We're going to be able to download our consciousness onto computers. Everyone in Silicon Valley is talking about it. Soon we'll all be able to live forever.

Silicon Valley is so full of shit.

If life extension is possible, she said, then I think we need to think differently about love. About sex, too. Monogamy will be one of the first things to go. We can't be expected to love one person for eternity.

What was I supposed to say now? I couldn't disagree with the future.

Have you taken new lovers? I asked.

That's a funny way of putting it. *Taken*.

Have you?

Two, she said. Then, unbidden, she named them: Roman and Jack. And then she described them. I don't remember what she said exactly. Short, tall, fat, skinny, blonde, brunette, rich and poor, smarter and funnier. I didn't like what she was saying, and I felt a sequence of sharp pangs which started in my thighs and shot up my whole torso, pointing toward my stomach.

Janice flicked her tongue around her mouth.

Night came on. Something clicked. I heard cars driving in the distance. I stood and turned off the light and lay down again next to Janice. Softly she stroked the wrinkles on my forehead with her thumbs. Your eyebrows look so crazy at night, she said, with the hairs going in all directions. She touched my cheekbones, the edges of my jaw.

Now Janice fell asleep—though I don't think she meant to—and I was awake, left to think about what had just happened. Janice and I, there, side by side, but in two different places.

Hours passed in darkness. I slept or didn't sleep or almost did, and suddenly there was a light on in the room and then in the hallway. A glow. I tried to sit up, to crank my neck and see where the light was coming from, but my body was weak and wouldn't rise. I tried again, again, but was caught in a continuous loop of effort and failure.

Again, the train horn rang.

Now Janice stood in front of me. This is how I knew she was going. I tried to speak to her, but couldn't. Couldn't move my lips. Couldn't but exhale the smallest breath. Where are you going? I wanted to say.

•

I must have fallen asleep because there it was, the

moon in the window like a searchlight pointing down. It was so pale that I thought of snow—was it snowing? Yes and no.

The phone was vibrating, a call, and I reached for it and answered. I raised my voice to speak clearly. Hello?

The voice on the other line said my name.

It's the middle of the night, I said.

My name again.

Who is this?

It's me, said the voice. Lawson.

Lawson?

Lawson, it said. Ezekiel.

(I had forgotten Lawson was Zeke's name.)

But you don't have a phone, I said. That's what you told me. You don't have a phone, didn't you tell me that?

The voice didn't answer. Where are you? it said.

Where am I? Where's Janice?

Are you home?

It's the middle of the night. Where's Janice?

I'm coming over, it said. I'm close by. Unlock the door. I don't want to have to knock. I don't want to wake anyone.

How do you know where I live?

It did not answer.

I pivoted and put my feet flat on the ground. Whose phone is this? I said.

Zeke had already hung up.

I stood and steadied myself and extended my hand and placed it against the wall and held myself up. I went to the front door and reached out to unlock it, but it was already unlocked. It was always unlocked. I shuffled back to my room and turned on the light. I dressed and got back in bed.

When Zeke came into my room, he went and sat at the desk chair. He did not speak. He was out of breath, and it worried me to see him like that. He cupped his hands and blew into them.

The smoke detector chirped in the hallway. There were voices outside my window seeming to imitate speech.

He placed himself in a thinking position. He looked more like a photograph than a man.

What are you doing here? Is Janice here?

He answered my question with a question. Can I trust you?

I thought I understood him. Course, I said. I'm not going to tell anyone about what happened.

He lifted his chin and the light hit him directly and I saw something in him I recognized. I knew what it was—something he had, I thought, tried to repress. I knew what it was because I lived it almost every day of my life. Fear. I knew it when I went to sleep and when I woke. I knew it so well that I had stopped experiencing it as fear and had come to understand it as something more ordinary—stress or purposelessness. But now that I saw it in him, I felt an intensification of it.

I need you to do something, he said.

Do what?

Those guys, they're trying to intimidate us.

Those same guys. And we can't back down.

Did something happen?

He put his hands up to his face and rubbed his cheeks and forehead and under his chin and around the back of his neck. Then he pulled off his hood and leaned back and crossed his legs. Neh, he went. Neh. Now he adjusted himself, fidgeting, and sat forward and leaned to the side and reached across his body into his back pocket. Now pulled it out slowly, the gun. The same as before. It was small, smaller than I remembered it. Almost like a toy.

Looking beyond me, toward the window, Zeke leaned back again and passed the gun from hand to hand and rotated it around his palm. He took the gun in his one hand and rested it on his knee. It pointed at me.

Don't point that fucking thing at me.

I shifted and turned away.

He set the gun on the floor and took off his sweatshirt. Then he picked up the gun again and held it loosely and set his hand on his knee. I need to know, he said, are you on our side? Things are going to get worse.

Things?

He picked up the gun again and pointed.

And it was then that he did it.

He pulled the trigger.

The gun clicked.

He pulled it again.

The gun clicked again. There was nothing more than that click, but when I heard it, I collapsed. I jolted back. The blank gunshot injected into me some shameful pleasure. And what came out of my mouth was not a word but a terrible laughter. It was completely involuntary. When I realized that I was laughing, I tried to stop, but the effort to stop only produced more laughter. I was hysterical. I fell back onto the bed and let it all out.

What are you laughing at?

My chest hurt, my face.

Now Zeke said what was obvious. The gun's empty, he said. It's always been empty.

I was laughing.

I need you to keep this for me, he said. But you don't need to worry about it because the gun is just a prop.

A prop, yeah.

He tossed the thing at me, and I turned to the side and let it fall beside me on the bed. It bounced and flipped and fell flat. When I told him that he was being ridiculous, he told me that I was being ridiculous.

Take responsibility, he said. We're in his fight together. For our future.

And now I felt lost in his slogans. And why was everyone always talking about the future all the time?

Now Zeke explained to me, in a voice completely serious, that I didn't need to *use* the gun, but that I needed to carry it, to be seen carrying it, to be known as someone who carries it. We must show them who we are. They ought to know we're not fucking around.

I noted his use of the word "we." I thought about the therapist—was this the same we?

I was surprised to be included in that we. I was part of a new collective. That's what I had wanted, wasn't it? It happened so fast that I couldn't understand how it happened, and I wasn't even completely sure who "we" were and what we were doing and why. And whether I wanted to go on being part of "we" seemed out of my control.

Antifa, I said. That's what you're talking about, right?

Zeke scrunched up his face like someone trying to wring water out of a sponge. Antifa? Antifa, no. No.

I didn't understand.

He pointed his finger at me. Now he pointed at the gun on the bed. Take it, he said. Pick it up.

I picked it up, the gun. I felt my hand fading beneath it, so that gun became a surrogate hand, a new means of touching the world. I gripped it. I pointed it at Zeke.

He liked that. He was pleased and he showed his teeth.

Do it, he said. Pull it.

My grip on the gun tightened and I squeezed the trigger slowly until I heard it click. I pulled again. It felt like nothing. It felt as natural and normal as lifting a glass of water to drink. I pulled it again and again and again. Over and over. So on and so forth. So many times, I lost count.

Zeke didn't flinch, didn't blink even.

Now he stood up and wiped his hands

together, and told me again that I needed to keep the gun and carry it with me. In a backpack or something. He told me that there was going to be a gathering at The Proletariat later that night and I ought to be there.

Ought. Who uses that word anymore?

When we shook hands goodbye, my pinky slipped between his pinky and his ring, and my thumb likewise slipped and landed in the divot between his pointer and his middle and made a tangle of fingers.

After he left, I turned off the light, and the room was dark again. The mini refrigerator clicked. Water sloshed inside the plastic jug.

35

I changed my clothes—jeans and an old North Face jacket with big pockets inside the zipper— and paced the room with the gun. I turned it over and tossed it around for a while and it scared me to be so casual with it.

Coffee was percolating in the machine.

That today was Election Day suddenly occurred to me. Soon the country would gather to vote to contribute to a future it may or may be able to understand.

The phone went. *Several people are trapped after a "major explosion" in Baltimore. The Great California Exodus: A look at why droves are leaving the state. Protests explode across the country; police declare several dead in Seattle and Portland, The US imposes its global "Do Not Travel" advisory.*

I flipped the switch and the overhead lights clicked on. The coffee settled. I rinsed my thermos out with what water I had left in the mini fridge and poured the coffee into it. Before I walked out of my room, I tucked the gun into the inside pocket of my jacket and waited until I couldn't hear my roommates and then opened my door to leave.

Turned out, I hadn't waited long enough because now, there, standing at the threshold was a woman I had never seen before. She was tall and her neck was long and she had a shaved head. She looked at me and smiled. Hi, her voice was small.

Hi, she said again. She pointed to my room. Do you live in there? In that room?

Me? Oh. Yeah, that's me.

We've been wanting to meet you, she said without hesitation.

She reached out to embrace me and we hugged the way strangers do, with the hips pulled back, leaning in with our shoulders so that our chests did not touch.

I'm Sam, she said. Hey, we're having a big breakfast today. It starts in about an hour. Big election day and all. For friends. You should come, if you want. Okay? People will be showing up in about two hours. There's a great community here. Lots of good people. There'll be mimosas and breakfast burritos and everything.

Breakfast burritos.

Hm-hm.

Vegan breakfast burritos?

Sure, yeah.

I told her I'd be there. Looking forward to it, I said. It will be great to meet you all, finally.

She agreed and smiled big and went her way down the hall and looked back and smiled again.

Alone again. I looked at the floor. What to do? I wanted to join. I think I wanted it. But I couldn't, I thought. Not right now. The timing was bad, unlucky. My mind was somewhere else, my body. I turned and shut the door and left.

•

Outside, the streets were empty, and my footsteps echoed against the sidewalk so that for a moment I thought I was being followed.

Why was I out here, again?

I figured I'd go out to walk because I wanted to see whether I could do it—whether I could be in public with the gun in my pocket, whether I had willpower for it. And now, as I walked, I thought about whether this walk alone could answer that question.

I took Telegraph. I knew where I was because of the smell. A thick, cool sea-mist infused with the stench of evaporating urine and asparagus and skunky, heady marijuana; the body odor of the now-invisible masses mingling with the tropical sweetness of surf wax—coconut and pineapple—and sunscreen and mandarin and rosemary leaf soap and fallen eucalyptus leaves and burning wood. I took a right on Bancroft and walked until I got to Piedmont and pushed on further past the football stadium onto Centennial Dr. and up into the hills. Finally, I stopped at the botanical gardens, which, other than a man sleeping beneath a row of scrawny bushes, were empty and quiet and still dark in the morning shade.

I sat for a long time. I tried to think. About love and guns and good causes, sex and politics, robots and suicide. I thought about Parker and Josh, my shepherd, and Benici and the therapist and Sam. I thought about the clown artist from the first novel I wasn't writing. I thought about Vernon. Franz. Simon. Jed. Gad. And all the novels I would never write.

Can you do this?

The phone went. *Russia is sounding the drum-beats of war, amassing troops near southern Ukrainian. The scientists behind the Doomsday Clock have warned, as the clock's 'time' was set for next year. India and China fail to defuse deadly border tensions. 'We thought that was the end': Afghan woman relives abduction by Taliban as she tried to flee the country. After too much chaos, one man packed his bags, quit his job, left the US, and moved to Mexico. Will others follow?*

Can you?

I made the decision then. Yes. I could do it, whatever Zeke had asked me to do. I would. Join the cause. Even if I didn't fully understand what the cause was. It would be better to live for something bigger than myself. To believe in something. And I would be my own Don Quixote and fight for a higher purpose. The future. I would carry the gun. Join Antifa. I would. And I did. Whatever doubts or fears I still had would vanish in time. And I would gain, eventually, some sense of fulfillment and gratification and purpose. And I would find meaning in resistance. And I would find friendship and inner peace in collectivity. I would have love, not romantic love, not with Janice, but somewhere.

From that vantage, I saw the entire Bay Area sprawling out across the brown, charred hills. The city undulated—the steelwork and the clocktower and the ranks of dilapidated buildings were reduced to rubble and debris. Rows of highways wound themselves around and surged up and along and down again, dropping into the valley where a thin layer of fog and smoke sat low.

Now, up ahead of me, there were flashing and flickering lights.

Heavy drums.

Buzzing insects.

It was a familiar feeling. A halo.

I looked at my broken wristwatch. But it was gone. Where was it? I must have taken it off. I began to panic. I thought to run home, but remembered I had a gun in my pocket and should calm down. Stay calm.

More heavy drums.

More buzzing insects.

My face was getting hot.

The taste of metal.

The smell of rotting meat.

And I had something like a vision. An alternate reality. It happened slowly. I saw myself. I was getting out. Leaving California. I saw myself throwing away everything I could lift. All my possessions. My books and notebooks, pens and paper, photographs and prints, computer and phone, clothing and collectables, whatever they were. My trash—mouthwash and body wash and aftershave and deodorant and cologne. I saw it. Now I was in my truck, retreating into the desert, back to Las Vegas, maybe, or farther down. Back to some crude origin. The air was clear. I saw my truck drifting along the empty highway. The desert around it proliferated, repeated. No evidence of civilization whatsoever. No future. No other ending. Nothing but the road. Dust and dirt. Sagebrush and mountains. Buzzing insects.

Taste of metal. Smell of rotting meat. The clouds billowed and unfurled and lured me on toward a single point where the road seemed never to end. I couldn't imagine anything else.

The sky was getting brighter. The sky was so bright I couldn't see the sky.

Acknowledgments

Thanks to: Emma Wood, Arel Wiederholt-Kassar, Micah Perks, James Yu, Karen Tei Yamashita, Lisa McKenzie, the Chicago Quarterly Review (where an excerpt of this novel was published), and especially Jon Roemer and Outpost19.

About the Author

Originally from Las Vegas, Dylan Bassett has lived many lives: a pastor in Russia, a semi-professional soccer player in Brazil, a translator in Kazakhstan, a local Democratic campaign manager in Utah, and now a professor of literature near Philadelphia. Bassett has an MFA from the Iowa Writers' Workshop and a PhD from the University of California-Santa Cruz.